A Posy o

Sharon Dempsey

Print ISBN 978-1-912604-41-8

Also By Sharon Dempsey

Little Bird - A serial killer thriller

Praise For Sharon Dempsey

"Sharon Dempsey writes with such warmth and affection it's hard not to be bowled over by her cast of characters as they deal with all life throws at them. Please tell me there will be a follow up and we will get to see what happens next? I think there is so much more to come from these women.

Sharon writes Belfast so well, I almost felt as if I was there and I could really picture myself in Moonstone and in the big house on Mount Pleasant Square. I'd love to sit with a cuppa in that back garden! I think this would make a fab TV series - it has so many heart-warming ingredients." – Claire Allan, Irish Times bestselling author of eight women›s fiction titles and new thriller release, Her Name was Rose.

For Jeannie and Teddy,
you both inspire me every day.

Chapter 1

*D*ating back to 1898, this handsome and individually designed house retains much of the original character, including decorative plasterwork to the ceilings, ornate mahogany staircase and sliding sash windows, and is set amidst mature gardens extending to circa half an acre.

The accommodation is of generous proportions and covers three floors, making it an excellent home for a growing family. On entrance, the wide hallway boasts the original wood block flooring, oak wood panelling, a cloakroom with high wall-mounted flush WC, pedestal wash hand basin, tiled floor, part-tiled walls and a built-in cupboard with ample space for storage.

The main drawing room offers an original marble fireplace with tiled hearth, inset and surround, picture rail, cornicing, and solid block wood floor. This room leads to a small bookcase-lined study with French patio doors to the side courtyard style garden.

The sitting room provides a view over the extensive rear gardens, with a window seating area, ceiling cornicing, fireplace with marble hearth, wood block flooring and door through to dining room.

Bedroom accommodation set out over two floors.

Master bedroom suite with period fireplace, separate dressing room and large en suite bathroom. Guest bedroom suite with separate sitting area and en suite shower room.

Two additional bedrooms on first floor and two further bedrooms are found on the second floor.

Outside there are exceptional gardens as well as a garage and ample parking. The property provides spacious family accommodation which retains many original characteristics and features, and is perfectly *complemented by the generous and private site with delightful level gardens to the rear along with a sheltered patio area with southerly aspect.*

Mount Pleasant Square is a mature leafy park off the popular Stranmillis Road and is recognised as one of the area's most sought after residential locations. It is situated in a conservation area, and undoubtedly Belfast's most desirable residential address. While this property enjoys considerable privacy and seclusion, the location could not be more convenient for access to Belfast City Centre, the vibrant Lisburn Road, main arterial routes, leading schools and academic institutions, parks and golf clubs.

Please note extensive modernisation required.

Ninety-seven Mount Pleasant Square. The address created a certain sense of contentment, as if to live there was to have reached a plateau of happiness and well-being.

Until that morning, when Ava received the estate agent particulars, she had it all sorted out in her head. She would sell up, pocket a mighty fortune and start her own business, or even go travelling, though she doubted she would go too far when she had her gran to consider. Realistically, Ava couldn't go backpacking around the south of Ireland let alone New Zealand, knowing her gran was languishing in the Sisters of Mercy nursing home.

The point was, that for the first time in her life, Ava had *possibilities*, choices which only a significant sum of money could provide. She felt like a Jane Austen heroine, thinking of how money could turn one's life around, except she didn't have to hunt down a man of good standing to secure her financial future. Financial security had sought her out, and might as well have fallen straight out of the sky onto her lap for all she knew of how it had come about.

The paperwork had stated that she was now the sole beneficiary of the estate which comprised of number ninety-seven. She had no way of establishing the reason why she had been left the house. She certainly didn't know of any rich relatives who would have left it to her and knew no reason why it should have remained a secret. It was unlikely her gran had known about the house, for surely, she would have told her that she had this inheritance to look forward to. Why had whoever owned the house chosen to neglect it and allow it to fall into such a poor sorry state? It was all a bit of a curiosity.

When she had received the initial letter requesting that she meet with Ms Boston of Hawkings Solicitors, Ava had assumed it was to do with her gran's affairs and her move to the nursing home. She had even prepared for the meeting by digging out the deeds of her gran's house along with social security numbers, her pension book and other such details.

The solicitor, a blonde elegant woman named Amanda, had expressed her delight at having tracked Ava down so easily. She had few details to go on, she explained. If Ava had moved, then the solicitor would have been stuck like a duck in a mudflat. She had extended her manicured hand to congratulate Ava on her good fortune, a diamond engagement ring winking in the sunlight as it cast prisms of light around the airless Ormeau Road office.

Ava sat there on the wine-coloured leather chair, dumbfounded, clutching the irrelevant paperwork, trying to process the information. A house? Left to her? Her initial reaction had been to assume that she had inherited the house from her mother. But firstly, as far as Ava knew, she hadn't died, and secondly, she hadn't visited Northern Ireland for many years, let alone owned a house here.

'Yeah, I can see it's a shock, but aren't you the lucky one?' Amanda had said, obviously happy to pocket the fee for tracking Ava down and finalising the details. It was clear to Ava that it wasn't every day that Amanda got to play the fairy godmother role. She was probably more used to dealing with Disability Living Allowance fraud cases and chasing up legal aid paperwork on behalf of good-for-nothing joyriders and recreational summer time rioters, hell-bent on throwing petrol bombs at the emergency services, fire brigade and ambulances included.

'This blue cardboard file has sat gathering dust for years. It must have been instructed well before my time,' Amanda said. 'Mr Hawking senior would have dealt with the original client way back in the seventies or eighties when the practice was in its heyday. We have a few leftover documents and cases to be tallied up from the days when Samuel Hawking ran the practice and this bequest file was one of them.'

Ava sat there, not really taking it all in, thinking that at some stage the solicitor would realise she had been mistaken and that she had the wrong Ava Connors. Ava could feel her skin prickle with the beginning of a heat rash – she always got over heated and itchy when she was nervous.

'But why now? And who left it to me?'

'All I can tell you is that the benefactor has requested that the house be signed over without disclosure of identity. Believe it or not, it isn't all that uncommon. Sometimes people don't wish for the whole world to know their business. You just got lucky.'

Amanda indicated with her heavy Waterman fountain pen where Ava should sign.

'I'll send an email confirming the transaction has been completed to the other lawyers acting on behalf of the benefactor. They made the initial contact with our office last month,' Amanda said, licking her poppy red lipsticked lips.

'Great, that is everything all nicely tied up,' she said.

Ava nervously pulled at her hair, leaving her unruly mane looking even more bedraggled than normal. 'What about things like inheritance tax, stamp duty?'

Amanda merely shrugged her narrow, navy pinstripe-suited shoulders. 'Technically it wasn't an inheritance, as such, more like a gift from a benefactor and so you needn't worry as that side of the transaction has been taken care of.' She smiled at Ava, flashing her professionally whitened teeth.

'And you are absolutely sure it's me the house has been left to? You haven't got the wrong person?'

'No doubt about it – Ava Connors, it's your lucky day. Hey, enjoy it. Celebrate and thank your lucky stars.'

Ava left the solicitor's office having agreed for Amanda to go ahead and have the house valued, with a view to putting it on the market. There was little point in keeping it, she reasoned. What was the point in rattling around in a big old house with Maggie in the nursing home? Ava wandered up towards University Street where she had parked her trusty Fiat Uno. A bluish streak of bird poop had splattered all over her window screen like a Jackson Pollock canvas. Maybe it was auspicious. Her gran always claimed that being shat on by a bird from above was a sign of good luck. Somehow, Ava couldn't see it as such, but today she felt like luck was on her side and, for a change, she was going to make herself enjoy it instead of fretting about it.

She threw her bag on the passenger seat and glanced at the address on the paperwork Amanda had given her. It wasn't so far. Her curiosity could barely be contained. It was one of those moments that she knew she should have been sharing with Finlay, her former boyfriend. He would have been beyond excited at the thought of them owning a big house, but this was something she now had to do alone.

Fifteen minutes later she peered through dense overgrown, snowberry hedging, its tangle of thickets almost preventing her from seeing much and was relatively unimpressed. Sure, number ninety-seven stood proud and imposing in its own way, but it did look tired and in desperate need of work and a good bit of money being spent on it. Money she didn't have.

The roof looked like it had warped under the strain of one too many harsh winters. The tall chimneys tilted slightly to the left, as if mimicking the leaning tower of Pisa, and the brickwork showed tell-tale signs of neglect where creepers had embedded the plaster, creating cracks. She didn't have the keys yet. Amanda had said it would be a couple of weeks before she could have them, but no one could stop her having a good nose around.

Now, sitting in the park a week later, reading the estate agent's spiel, her heart sank like a pebble in a pond. Ava was used to feeling that life was safe, steady, and most of all predictable. She didn't seek the thrills of unknown situations or crave excitement. She was one of life's contented few. But accepting that this house was truly hers for the taking, and that she could move into it, seemed to be asking for trouble. The gods of fate would look down and see that life had thrown Ava Connors a surprise and welcomed bonus and would seek out ways to disrupt her equilibrium. Not that she truly believed in all that carry on. It was more a sense of feeling that life would be different if she moved into number ninety-seven, and although that may not have been a bad thing, she was wary about what it *could* mean. She wasn't one to go looking for change, so when it came her way, her natural inclination was reluctance to allow it to unfurl.

Perhaps it's time I allowed myself a wee bit of excitement, she thought enjoying the weak warmth of the sun on her skin.

Sometime between receiving the solicitor's letter detailing the transfer of ownership to Ava and receiving the estate agent's folder, the house had begun to take on a significance, a character all of its own. She no longer saw it as an escape route to something else, easy money to pave her way in life, removing her from everything she was used to and comfortable with, but rather more like a sanctuary. On one hand, she admonished herself for being so sentimental. She was allowing the estate agent speak to sell the house to her.

But then again, someone wanted her to have it and perhaps there was a good reason she had yet to discover. It was a lovely warm feeling to think that someone, somewhere, had decided that Ava Connors should be bestowed such a grand house, no matter how run down and sad it looked.

How it had come to be in her name was all part of the mystery. Her gran, really her only family to speak of, had never been comfortably well off, let alone wealthy. She had struggled to earn every penny. So why, if she had possession of such a large house in a prestigious postcode, had she not either sold up and lived off the profit or lived in it? Instead, whoever had owned the house had left it to grow mouldy and rot, as if it were waiting for Ava to turn up.

Ava brushed a few crumbs off her lap for the birds to eat and threw her cardboard cup in the bin. She felt lighter to have made the decision, as if somehow, she had been expected to do so all along but she needed to go through the motions of sounding out the alternatives to herself.

It had a certain allure, not just because of the exclusive post code or the grandeur of the square in which it sat. Ava was drawn to it like a magnet. She felt some familial connection with it; one which she was willing to nurture like a baby plant sprouting from a bud on the stem of a dendrobium orchid.

Chapter 2

'Got the keys!' Ava all but squealed with excitement down the phone to Niamh.

'Can't believe I'm stuck in Dublin. Can't you wait until I'm home and we can go together?' Niamh pleaded. She was on a film job, but Ava knew even the thought of pressing mineral powder on Cillian Murphy's brow wasn't enough to stop her longing to accompany Ava on her first proper viewing of the house.

'No way. You'll have to wait. I'm about to head there now.'

'Let me know every detail and pick a lovely room for me to stay in.'

'Niamh, I still haven't decided for sure if I'm keeping it.'

'Of course, you'll keep it, you lucky cow. Good luck. Gotta go, the catering truck has pulled up and if I time it right I might get to eat my dinner with Cillian.'

Ava placed her phone back in her bag and smiled. Niamh had been good to her those last few weeks as she tried to get over her heartbreak. Everyone agreed Finlay Kane was a good catch. You would need to be dead from the waist down not to fancy him, as Niamh often liked to tell Ava. There was no denying his obvious appeal: six feet one, a good head of thick brown hair that showed no hint of thinning or greying, dark, almost menacing eyes which twinkled like fairy lights when he laughed and a body, hard and broad, obtained through regular training sessions to feed his passion for playing Gaelic football. No, certainly, no one could deny he wasn't a good catch on paper.

Everyone, except Ava, that is.

Then, just when Ava thought he might be in the throes of proposing, he went and broke up with her, making Ava realise that what she had with Finlay was something special.

'I'm sorry, Ava,' he had said, 'but there isn't any point in hanging on in there. You just don't light up for me.' He continued, his voice soft and low with emotion, 'Maybe I'm wrong, but I think I haven't had the best of you and that someone, somewhere, will. I wish them well and I'm sorry it can't be me, but there it is.'

'Don't be ridiculous. You sound like Niamh; expecting fireworks with every kiss. This is real life, Finlay, not some romantic film. Sparks don't happen after eight years of being together.'

'Be honest, Ava, it wasn't exactly fireworks at dawn at the beginning either. I thought you were reserved and shy, but try as I have, I haven't been able to warm you up.' He began eating his fried slices of chorizo covered in peppers and garlic. How could he eat when he was slowly strangling her heart?

Ava impaled a chilli prawn with unnecessary force and wondered why she felt so tragically sad. Most of what Finlay had said was true, so why did she feel cheated and bereft?

'I just think we should take a break and see other people. Life is too short to settle for second best and I don't want to be your second best, Ava.'

She couldn't deny what he was saying was true. Perhaps there was something missing. But if you had never experienced it, how did you know? She had no relationship experience to compare notes. Maybe she did need to play the field a little. The truth was, the thought of being single and looking for love scared the bejaysus out of her. Finlay was used to going out with his mates and doing the club scene. Ava would prefer to curl up with a good crime novel and a big bar of Whole Nut, or to be sending funny cat pictures to her far-away friend, Joseph.

She would waste away in Moonstone Street, the little terrace house she had shared with her gran, and cat Lulu, until Maggie had gone into the Sisters of Mercy nursing home, never to have a boyfriend again. To find love was to go out and actively look for it, and Ava hadn't a clue when it came to playing those sorts of dating games. God, the thought of Tinder made her shudder. She didn't flirt, didn't know how to, and as for tarting herself up, it all seemed mildly absurd.

The unexpected windfall of the house on Mount Pleasant Square had helped to soothe her bruised heart. Niamh's enthusiasm for the house was infectious. Instead of worrying about the ins and outs of who bequeathed it to her, and trying to fret over the renovations, Niamh was just plain excited for her, and Ava decided that it was high time she felt the same, even if it was going against her natural disposition.

She couldn't help it, she was a worrier, but she had always been happy in her own skin. She never understood when her school friends pinched an inch of flesh and groaned because they could. She didn't long to have blonde hair when she had mid-brown hair the same shade as nutmeg, and she never pined to be doing something she wasn't.

Life was just fine as it was. Comfortable, secure, sheltered even. She never went looking for excitement and it usually never came looking for her. Maybe that was part of the problem; she was just content to *be*.

Listening to Niamh, Hazel, — her boss — and others chatter on about life and aspirations, Ava was often aware of how much they tried to look into the future. They were crystal ball gazers looking out for that next big thing in their lives. It was as if they expected something out there to be bigger and better and coming their way. Ava had always been happy just to be waking up in Moonstone Street with Maggie for company and the pleasure of working with beautiful flowers in a shop which kept her busy but not stressed, earning enough money to get by.

She thought of Joseph, her old friend and former neighbour. While Ava and Niamh had attended the Catholic grammar school, Joseph went to the nearby Protestant one. His world was rugby and rowing, running with the fast girls from Malone Grammar, and even though they moved in different circles, they always remained close.

Growing up, Ava and Joseph spent many hours playing Scrabble and Cluedo at their houses in Moonstone Street. But when Joseph went off to university in Liverpool to study software programming and design, and then landed a job in San Francisco, Ava remained at home. Even though his life seemed exciting, she always had the feeling that he had never really stopped wanting to return home. She was one of the lucky ones who knew the value of being happy with her lot.

So, for Ava to find herself driving along the Malone Road, looking for the left turn into Mount Pleasant Square to view a house which had been predetermined, by someone she didn't know, to belong to her, she was just a little bit on the queasy side. She didn't do mysteries. Niamh on the other hand would have thrived in this circumstance. The sensation of nausea snaking its way around Ava's belly would have been described by Niamh as butterflies, little flits of excitement in the pit of her stomach. But Ava wasn't like Niamh, and rather than feel elation at the prospect of owning a home of substantial standing, Ava was quite honestly petrified. There was no point doing a Miss Marple and trying to work out the identity of the generous benefactor or the "Sugar Daddy" as Niamh insisted on calling him; if he or she wanted to be known to her then Ava was pretty sure she would have known by now.

Until the paperwork had been finalised, she couldn't claim possession, but once Amanda has sorted out the legalities, Ava had been finally allowed to take official ownership. She had called into Amanda's office at lunchtime to pick up the keys, sick with anticipation. The keys had sat all afternoon in her bag, tormenting her with curiosity. She had been busy at work, so she had been able to cope most of the day, but come five o'clock she was out of Blooming Dales as fast as she could run.

Ava pulled up outside the house and allowed herself a moment to take in the scene. The square was a large stretch of well-maintained lawn edged with copper beech trees around which the houses had been built. The area had a hushed atmosphere that only serious money could buy. Ava was sure her neighbours would be high-end professionals: doctors, barristers and company directors — all with wealth and a certain sense of privilege.

What was she doing in possession of such a house? It seemed mildly ludicrous that she should have come into ownership of a home which was probably worth more than she could ever make in a lifetime as a shop assistant in a florist.

Still, someone wanted her to have it and she was more than intrigued as to why. Everyone had come under scrutiny – Mr Harris, a regular customer to Blooming Dales, and his kindly attachment to Ava was suddenly questioned. Had he died and left the house to her? Or the original owners of the florists, Esther and Harold? They were wealthy; had they, out of some sense of loyalty, left it to her? She even looked at the postman strangely to see if he knew some dark secret about her parentage which could explain it all.

Locking up her car she couldn't shake a sense of déjà vu. She had thought of practically nothing else but this house and Finlay for the past two weeks, so it was probably no more than her mind playing tricks on her. She had envisaged this moment, tried to imagine what the house would look like inside and now, here she was, about to put form, shape and colour to her imaginings.

The tall, iron, rusty gates of number ninety-seven were padlocked but Ava held the keys. They felt weighty and potent in her pocket. She fumbled with the bundle to identify the corresponding key for the lock on the gates. It clicked in and she partly lifted and pushed the heavy gates back into the overgrown drive, while simultaneously shoving a branch of berberis red leaf hedge out of her face, and made her way up the drive — feeling trepidation course through her veins.

What if the house was overrun with mice, or worse, rats? It was bound to be damp and crawling with spiders never mind the thought of ghosts lurking around corners. Her heart thundered out a rhythm like the clatter of wild horses.

She wished she had told Finlay about the house before the break up. She could have asked for his company, but something made her want to keep the house all to herself. Just until she got her head around the enormity of it. Besides, she hadn't wanted Finlay getting any ideas about settling down and proposing now that she was the owner of such a grand family home. Not that he would be after her for her inheritance; it was just that seeing such a home would make anyone think of settling down and breeding a nest of children to fill the many vacant rooms. Still, look where that line of thinking had got her. The joke was most definitely on her.

For the past few nights, she had tossed and turned in bed, one-minute feeling bereft that she no longer had Finlay in her life, and the next mulling over what the house would look like. As she lay in her single bed in Moonstone Street, staring at the twee pink and sage green floral wallpaper Maggie had chosen many years earlier, she was glad to have the distraction of number ninety-seven to stop her obsessing over Finlay. Having the house to think about, and visualising its layout, had stopped her falling into a self-pitying crying session.

She had managed to hold off telling Joseph. He'd be delighted about her house news, but she felt pathetic to be reporting her relationship status. Joseph, like Niamh, had made something of his life. While Ava was letting hers pass her by, he had headed off to university and ended up in Silicon Valley, in a job she couldn't even begin to comprehend.

Standing on the front driveway surveying the scale of the house and the grounds, she felt like a little girl gazing into her future, imagining what might be. Strangely enough, she felt as though she had stepped into a dream. Reading and rereading the estate agent's descriptions had given her a sense of the layout and the features in each of the rooms, but it wasn't enough to read the descriptions. She wanted to see the proportions of the rooms, to feel the sunlight stream through the windows onto her face, to listen to the sounds of the birds in the overgrown gardens, and to sense what the house could mean to her.

The garden was an abundance of colour and fat willowy blooms with nature taking advantage to flourish in the absence of restraint. Tall violet foxgloves and orange great reedmace flanked the path with dandelions underfoot and hawthorn bursting through at every opportunity.

The front door was painted a dark green, but the paint was splitting and peeling. The brass knocker and the ninety-seven brass plaques were tarnished and mottled. Ivy crawled up the sides of the doorway like creepers in a horror movie, as if protecting the house from intruders. A collection of cracked and tawdry terracotta pots were clustered around the three wide steps leading up to the door, but whatever they had held had shrivelled and died long since, giving way to a collection of dandelions, weeds and moss.

Ava walked up the stone steps. This was a momentous occasion. The fear and the anxiety she had felt melted away, and suddenly she experienced all the excitement and trepidation of a new bride being carried over the threshold, except she had no groom to do the carrying. But there was a sense of starting out, that this was the beginning of something. An image of James Stewart and Donna Reed in *It's a Wonderful Life* popped into her head. She could remember the scene of their old falling down house, and how their faces, lit by the moon, had glowed with excitement at what their future could hold while they sang, *By the Light of the Silvery Moon*.

Ava almost laughed at herself for her romantic notions. She was the most unromantic and least sentimental person really, but this house had caught her imagination and made her tingle with goosebumps.

It was a wide doorway, its proportions in keeping with the size of the house. Ava worked her way through the keys until she found the one most likely to fit the front door. She held out her hand with the key poised in the keyhole, slightly shaking at the thought of what lay behind the big green door. She was all a flutter with a nervous energy, which made her feel like running and jumping just for the sake of it like a five-year-old on Smarties. Opening the door and knowing she was about to see the interior at last was like unwrapping the best present ever, and Ava hardly ever received presents which she hadn't chosen in advance.

At last, she stood in the oak panelled hallway and surveyed the scene. It was a grand entrance with parquet flooring, dulled by dust and time, with a wide staircase leading to a tall, narrow, stained-glass window on the first-floor landing. The light streamed in through the coloured glass creating a kaleidoscope on the threadbare, moth-eaten, carpeted stairs. Dust motes danced in the light like microscopic fairies while the whole house seemed to sigh in response to having a long-waited-for visitor. Four panelled doors, all closed, led off from the hallway.

Ava decided to go to the right first and turned the Bakelite handle of the first door. She walked through and found a large, square-shaped living room, dominated by a tall, ugly fireplace of brown and grey marble. Picture rails lined the walls leading to a large deep bay window that looked out over the front gardens. A set of French doors led to the side of the house. Branches of a lilac tree in full vibrant bloom pushed against the French doors as if nosing in to see who was wandering around the old, long-neglected house.

Ava sighed. It was a beautiful room that even dirt, dust and cobwebs couldn't disguise. The high ceiling and the proportions of the space created a welcoming area, which even though it was so large and empty of furniture, still seemed cosy and inviting.

She moved on through to a connecting door and found herself in what was probably a dining room or breakfast room. It too had French doors, rusty, with dark green mildew lurking in the corners of the metal frames. The doors looked out onto a small crazy-paved courtyard with emerald green velvety moss growing in between the cracks.

The kitchen was to the back of the house and consisted of an assortment of mustard colour Formica cupboards set off with turquoise tiles on the walls which screamed circa 1970s. A creamy buttermilk-coloured painted Welsh dresser took up one wall and an alcove of shelves nestled in the corner with enough room for a table and chairs and even a small sofa.

Ava tried the back door and heard something scurry away under the partially rotted wooden frame. Urgh, she hated mice.

She would be glad to have Lulu. She smiled as she was already picturing herself curled up with a book in the corner of the kitchen with her pretty, arrogant cat at her feet.

The back door opened up onto a utility area where a broom and an old rusty mangle stood looking forlorn. She moved on through the back door to see the gardens. They were a wild, overgrown jungle of lupins, climbing roses, a huge gooseberry bush, heavy with fruit, tall purple-headed chives and a mass of lavender. The lawn had become a patchwork of dandelions and clover while the remaining grass was windswept and overgrown. A paved path snaked through the growth but was largely disguised by moss and the tangled branches of some unidentifiable shrub which had rejoiced in the lack of regular pruning. The garden was edged by three tall trees, one an apple tree, the other which looked like a plum, and a grand sycamore. Overgrown hedging stood behind the trees creating complete privacy.

Ava made her way back into the house. She still had two downstairs rooms to explore never mind the upstairs. Although the house had been clearly empty for a long time, it didn't smell of damp. Instead, Ava thought she could smell lavender as she climbed the stairs. A faint smell of lavender mixed with dust and old newspapers.

Each stair creaked and groaned under her weight, making her feel certain that if she were to be lying in bed, no one could ever tiptoe up to the bedrooms without her hearing them. She stopped at the first-floor landing beneath the grimy stained-glass window and looked down onto the hallway. It was a gorgeous house, very grand yet homely and would obviously make a fabulous family home.

Maybe Ava was crazy to consider living in it. What would she do knocking around in such a big house all on her own? It wasn't as if she had Maggie to share it with and Finlay had made his feelings clear. He had almost certainly moved on. Maybe Ava was destined to become an old spinster living with Lulu, the cat, in the big house. The local kids would play "Belfast" — ring her door bell and run — fearful of the nasty old lady who lived all alone with her cat for company.

The rational response would have been to sell it. Even though the housing market had crashed in Northern Ireland following a period of crazed buying and selling in response to the new state of peace, Ava was sure such a house in a much sought-after location would sell. Perhaps for not as good a price as she would have got a couple of years earlier but realistically she could probably get half a million easily, even in such a bad state of repair.

But what would she do with so much money? The thought of travelling may have appealed to her when she was younger, but she couldn't bear the thought of leaving Maggie. And starting up her own business didn't really make sense. What would be the point, just to earn more money to buy another house somewhere else?

Her mind was racing with ideas and she wished yet again that she had Finlay to share it with. Still, at least Niamh would be delighted for her and the two of them could spend hours discussing layouts and drooling over interior design magazines. Hazel would be a great help too and would definitely have an opinion on every Farrow and Ball paint sample. Ava couldn't just move in overnight. There was still a lot to consider, not least the work which would need doing.

It was surreal to think that she owned it. Ava Connors, who had never imagined living in such a house, could simply pack a suitcase, a few clothes, books and stuff, and she could be good to go. She had no real reason to stay in Moonstone Street beyond a sense of loyalty to Maggie and a fear of uprooting Lulu. The biggest problem preventing her from making the leap was that from the outside, the house, appeared to be in a sad state of repair. 'Wreck and ruin' was the expression Maggie would have used. Without having a builder's discerning eye, Ava couldn't really assess the full picture, but it was unlikely to be habitable without a lot of hard graft and a fair poke of money. The hard graft wouldn't be a problem, Ava would happily throw on a headscarf and a pinny to strip wallpaper and sand down floors, but she had a sneaky suspicion the house would be in need of a more substantial makeover, requiring expertise and cash — neither of which she could claim to have. Where she would manage to find the necessary spondulicks to do the house up was another problem she had avoided thinking too deeply about.

She was frustrated that she couldn't talk to Maggie about it. She longed to settle down at their kitchen table with Nambarrie tea leaves stewing in the brown teapot and a plate of ginger snap biscuits at the ready to be dunked into their mugs while they mulled over the whole episode. Part of her felt that it would have been unfair to tell Maggie about it. Anything out of the ordinary upset her and it would be a sure sign that Ava was considering life beyond Moonstone Street.

Still, part of Ava couldn't help think this house had to be linked in some way to her gran. Part of her reluctance to tell Maggie was related to her fear of damaging their relationship. She didn't want to feel anger or hurt as a result of Maggie not sharing something so big with her. It was the way she had always been with her gran.

Then there was Maggie's usual resistance to anything grand. Ava was sure Maggie would give one of her looks, indicating that to own such a house was to reject all she had been brought up to value. Maggie mistrusted wealth and she would consider Mount Pleasant Square to be an insult to her very being. Ava could imagine Maggie's mouth twisting into a sneer of disapproval and she didn't want to risk that.

Ninety-seven Mount Pleasant Square was meant to be Ava's house and she loved the idea of it becoming her home. Now that she felt there was no reason why she shouldn't own the house, and possibly live there, she was thinking of a million ways to make it happen.

Joseph, you'll never guess what's happened. I've only gone and inherited a big old, falling down house!

What? For real?

Yep.

That's fantastic. Couldn't happen to a nicer girl. Hang on, who died?

That's the strange thing. I don't know. Weird eh?

How can you inherit a house without knowing who left it to you? Surely the solicitor will know.

She says that it has been "bequeathed" to me. Don't think we've ever had that word on the Scrabble board.

So, what are you doing with this old house?

That's part of the mystery. I think I know and then, the next time I think about it, I don't know. One minute I decide to sell it, and the next I'm daydreaming about moving in. Wish you were here to sort me out. You know what Niamh is like. God, I love that girl, but her mind is nearly always on some fella.

Keep me posted. I'm about to go into a conference to give a presentation on Computational Methods for Simulation of Biological Development.

Ah, Joseph, here's me wittering on about my mystery house and you're in the middle of something really important.

No big deal. There are only two hundred or so people out there. Waiting on me. Shit. I've just managed to make myself nervous.

Take a big breath in. You'll do brilliantly. I know you will.

Thanks, Ava. Can I breathe out yet?

Sure. Now, go get them.

Chapter 3

'Girl, dry your eyes and catch yerself on. No man is worth ruining your mascara over,' Cal, Niamh's work friend was in full flow, determined to sort out Ava's heartache. She clenched her jaw and let him continue. Once he started there was no holding him back. Best to ride the wave, until she reached the shore.

'When I was dumped by Malachy the Boke, I gurned for days. All that achieved was to dry out my skin and make my eyes look piggy-small. Believe me, it took a half bottle of fifty quid serum to restore my skin to its natural glow.'

'What you need is a night out,' said Niamh, rescuing Ava from a blow by blow account of Cal's lost loves, 'and I don't mean a trip to the cinema and a quick drink in The Errigle on the way home. A proper night out, let's do the *scene*!' She said it like there was something salacious and wonderful to be had out there, in club land, that place which came alive at midnight with weird and suspicious characters all out for a good time.

'Yes, let's,' said Cal. 'We can take you to all the best clubs on the scene and give you a proper night out.'

'The scene? What scene?' asked Ava, full of trepidation. The scene for Niamh and Cal could be the gay scene, an S&M house party or a weekend of drug taking and debauchery with suburban swingers from Edenderry.

'Don't worry, nothing too scary for a novice like yourself. I was thinking we could go to the burlesque night down in Macy's Basement.' Niamh was painting her toenails a lurid mauve colour while Ava was drinking coffee. She had called into Niamh's apartment on the way back from visiting Maggie at the nursing home.

The debris of Niamh's previous night out lay strew across the living room. A pair of black patent spiked killer heels were discarded on the floor along with a short denim skirt, and a spangled black top, the sleeve of which was partially draped over a half-empty cereal bowl. The dregs of the cereal were cemented to the sides of the bowl like concrete.

Not for the first time, Ava wondered how on earth she and Niamh managed to remain friends. They had so little in common, but somehow it didn't matter. She loved Niamh's sense of adventure and spontaneity even if it was far removed from Ava's own safe personality.

'Here, do your toes while you're sitting there.' Niamh indicated to the box of nail varnish sitting on the floor. Ava opened it and peered in, trying to decide which colour she should use. There in front of her was a manifestation of the difference between them. Ava had two bottles of nail varnish at home: one a pale shell pink and the other one clear. Niamh's collection was like a riot in a Smarties factory. Luminous yellows, candy pinks, and electric blues, nothing sedate and boring like nude or French pink. Opting for a rather flamboyant raspberry sorbet shade, she pulled off her fluffy grey socks and painted her toes. Despite Ava's lack of interest in all things sparkly and girly, they had been friends since before forever, having bonded over a box of crayons in Miss Archer's primary two class, that and a dark secret which had bound them together ever since.

One lunchtime Miss Archer had noticed that Niamh was looking a bit peaky, so she told her she could spend the lunch hour in the warmth of the classroom rather than hanging around the frost-covered playground. Ava was allowed to accompany Niamh and the two of them thought they were great, getting to have the whole classroom to themselves.

Unfortunately, in all the excitement of playing with the blackboard and impersonating Miss Archer, Niamh had a little accident resulting in a puddle at the top of the classroom. Rather than admit she had wet herself, Niamh and Ava set about drying it up with none other than Miss Archer's purple mohair cardigan which had been conveniently draped over her chair.

They had sat shame faced throughout the rest of the school day, in mortal fear of Miss Archer feeling the cold and putting on the cardigan. Thankfully, if she had discovered that her cardigan, hand knitted during the previous term, was mysteriously damp, it occurred when Ava and Niamh were safely at home watching the Clangers and eating their tea.

The incident ensured that they would always be friends, bound as they were by the laden guilt which had lingered like the stench of warm pee, long after Miss Archer had knitted a new cardigan. They had remained friends even when they had grown up and developed interests beyond Abba records, Johnny Depp posters and making pom-poms out of cast-off balls of wool as shown on Blue Peter.

Usually, Ava never bothered with make-up. She didn't see the point of all that gunk and whale blubber to tart yourself up and fool some poor fella into thinking he was pulling someone with Slavonic cheekbones and arched eyebrows. Niamh's trade was make-up, and so she was into all that shading and contouring and hiding her true Irish colouring. Ava preferred to be low maintenance. She had a wash-and-go routine in the morning: a quick shower and a rough towel dry of her tawny brown hair, and she was ready. Sure, no one passed any remark when you were stood behind a counter all day up to your elbows in raffia, oasis and lilies.

Maybe having raspberry toes would liven Ava up and give her a bit of sparkle.

Ava loved Niamh's effortless style and lust for life. Niamh was one of those girls who did her own thing. She made unusual look quirky and girly look feminine. She also possessed an outrageously large collection of shoes and knee-high boots and lots of funky handbags and a market-stall worth of beads, pearls and sparkly jewels, which Ava loved to rummage through. She also had the face of a mischievous elf teamed with the body of a woodland nymph.

Men loved her combination of effortless fun and not giving a hoot about anything, and Ava could see why.

Her apartment was an extension of her riotous personality; full of edgy prints and glitzy furnishings. If asked about her thoughts on the hot pink backdrop to Niamh's ultra-modern kitchen-dining area, Ava would have struggled to find a good description to say without causing offence. Bright, fun, loud would have been the best she could have come up with, but really it just seemed mildly ridiculous to Ava. It made her want to wear sunglasses and she couldn't imagine living with it, let alone having to face it with a hangover. Still, she couldn't help admire Niamh's individuality and her self-expression.

The electric blue shower room was certainly interesting, with the silver disco ball hanging above the loo, and the bedroom decorated in black and white Rococo style was like something out of a film set. Love it or loathe it, there was no denying Niamh had a certain style and flair.

'What's the craic with Joey? Any flirty little text messages from San Fran?' Niamh asked with one eyebrow arched.

'He hates when you call him Joey and no, we don't do flirty text messages. I've told you before, we're just good friends.'

Cal rolled his eyes dramatically. 'Girl, men don't do friendship. They have two speeds — sex and not sex. You'd do well to take note.'

'I've known Joseph for years. He's the boy next door, nothing else.' She had to admit she missed Joseph. When he headed off to Liverpool for university, she had always expected him to come back when his degree was finished, but a job offer in Silicon Valley had been too good to turn down.

'If I'd a mate in San Fran I'd be busting a gut to get a freebie holiday,' Cal said. 'I'd love to see it. Great clubs and everything.'

'I couldn't leave Maggie. Maybe one day,' Ava said.

Niamh sighed. 'Ava Connors, one day won't wait for you.'

Ava needed a bit of Niamh to rub off on her, now more than ever. Some of that kookiness and her exuberant love of life and that sense of adventure could help her get over Finlay.

'All right, I can't go to San Francisco, but I will go to this here burlesque thingy, but the deal is you help me get ready for it. Not a makeover, mind, just let me a have a rummage through your wardrobe and you can do my make-up,' Ava said feeling brave. She had agreed, despite her inherent reservations, but there was no point going half-heartedly. She might as well look the part.

'Yeah!' screamed Niamh, nearly knocking over her bottle of nail varnish, 'I've been itching to do you over for years, Ava Connors. Don't worry about a thing. Finlay Kane will be begging you to take him back by the time I'm finished with you.'

'Steady on. I said you could help me get dressed up, not remodel me like I'm the bionic woman or a TOWIE wannabe. I don't want anything too drastic,' Ava warned, but barely concealed a giggle, for no one could resist Niamh's infectious love for playing dress up.

There was a time when Ava wasn't so dowdy and boring. She had worn short skirts and pixie boots, slicked on cherry-flavoured lip gloss and had done the club scene with Niamh, but it was more youth club than night club. When she was seventeen, a mere baby, Niamh had dragged her out most Saturdays to shop for an outfit — usually some ensemble from Miss Selfridge or Exhibit — and then they would go back to Niamh's house to put it all together, telling each other they looked 'class'.

It was all so innocent. A Bacardi and coke or vodka and orange juice, a drag on a cigarette if someone was passing one around, and a quick snog on the dance floor as she was rocked to George Michael in the arms of some wee lad with yellow-headed spots and bum fluff on his top lip.

Niamh had moved on and progressed to rave nights, proper students' parties with scenes of wanton lust going on in spare bedrooms, while Ava had been happy to watch the telly with her gran and have Scrabble nights with her mate Joseph. She never felt she was missing out but, looking back, she couldn't help think that perhaps a vital part of her growing up had been lost. Maybe everyone needed to go through that period of teenage rebellion and trying on different personalities for size before settling into who they really were.

Later that night, Ava was driving home from Niamh's when she had found herself turning onto Annadale Embankment and towards where Finlay lived. It was as if she were on autopilot and had been summoned by the gods of fate.

Ava turned the engine off and sat trying to look inconspicuous. Finlay lived in Jerusalem Street which consisted of a row of terrace houses not unlike her own on Moonstone Street. The streets of the area were edged by the banks of the River Lagan, a dawdling and murky river which ran through the city.

Ava sank down as low as she could into her seat, not wanting to be seen. The streetlight directly opposite his house was broken, probably smashed by a hurling ball, so she was lucky enough to be in darkness, save for the moonlight which was casting a silvery pale glow over the wet street. A light, drizzly rain was falling softly but she didn't put on her wipers. Instead she sat, waiting.

God, this is like stalkerville, she thought. Niamh would laugh at her for being so soft. She didn't know what she wanted. Would it help to speak to Finlay and try to reason why they had ended? She thought not. They both knew the reason lay with Ava and it was up to her to sort herself out. In the past, whenever Finlay had brought up the subject of marriage, Ava had readily humoured him without ever actually committing to any formal arrangement. It wasn't like he had proposed, as such, more just sussing her out in advance of the big question. They talked about it in generalised terms; something to be considered in the future, not a pressing issue. A small part of her conscience thought that it was unfair to keep the poor man living in hope, but she didn't want to burn her bridges either.

But she knew marriage was expected. He came from a family of four happily married sisters who had a ready supply of flower girls and page boys all waiting for the opportunity to trot up the aisle, scattering rose petals at their new auntie's feet. Ava didn't feel ready to be gliding up any aisle just yet. Rose petals could wait. Sure, she was only young, not yet thirty.

Then there was the whole baby dilemma to worry about. Marrying Finlay would have come with the express expectation to be an instant breeder. Finlay adored every one of his nieces and nephews. Just as everyone thought he was a great potential husband, they also considered him to be ideal father material. He thought nothing of changing nappies and burping newborns over his shoulder, looking like he was made for being a daddy. But try as hard as she had, Ava couldn't visualise herself as a mummy. Not in this lifetime.

Hazel, her boss, had suggested the reason for Ava's aversion to mothering, lay in Ava's lack of a relationship with her own mother. But how could she explain to Hazel that Maggie had been more of a mother to her than she could ever have hoped for? There was certainly nothing lacking in Maggie's mothering skills, and so what if her actual mother had been AWOL for almost all of her childhood? She probably wouldn't have been as caring or loving as Maggie had been, even if she had stayed around. All in all, Ava was sure she had the better deal in being brought up by her grandmother instead of her flighty, runaway mother.

Maybe there was something in Hazel's psychobabble, but Ava couldn't help how she felt. Mind you, listening to Hazel go on about her kids was enough to put anyone off. If being a mother was so wonderful, Hazel did an excellent job disguising the fact. An hour of listening to her go on about her four-day labours, never mind the problems she had with her eldest son Daniel's school, would have been a far better contraception than any amount of teenage sex education lectures.

Her train of thought was broken when she heard a car's engine and saw the headlights dance off the road as it pulled up to Finlay's house.

Shit, shit, shit. Ava tried to shimmy lower down into her seat. She didn't want a confrontation. If she needed to talk to him she could have rung his mobile, but this was too much like being caught out waiting on him, spying even.

His car door clunked shut and she watched as he moved round to the passenger side to open the door. Ava gasped, her heart missing a beat as she realised he wasn't alone. Desperate now not to be seen, but too shocked and curious to move away, she watched as a tall blonde girl poured herself out of the bucket seat in one fluid movement. Willowy was the word to describe her. She pulled her cream-coloured trench coat up over her head to shield her long hair from the rain, as Finlay put a protective arm around her waist, steering her towards his front door.

In that instant, Ava's heart felt like it had been inflicted with a million tiny paper cuts. It lunged from a sorrowful longing to a raging jealousy, as she watched the man she was supposed to be with, be with touch another woman.

'My life is falling apart,' she murmured to no one but herself. She sniffed, feeling a wave of self-pity welling up, and threatening to spill out into self-loathing.

She waited, terrified that the bedroom light would switch on. She could picture them climbing the stairs, their hands pulling greedily at each other's clothes. Suddenly there he was. Finlay Kane lit up like a film star on the big screen reaching to pull the curtains closed, before he went off to his appreciative co-star to partake in the performance of the night.

There was ever only one thing to do when Ava felt miserable: text Joseph. He could always make her smile and help her see that even if life wasn't all daisy chains and sunshine, it was still worth smiling.

Ava: *Joseph, it's me.*

Joseph: *Bout ye, Ava. How's it going?*

Ava: *Grand, how's you?*

Same old. Working hard. They say New York is the city that never sleeps, but I think San Fran beats it hands down. I'm pulling all-nighters here.

Ava: *Joseph Delaney, you've got to slow down. Haven't you heard that you can burn out by the time you're thirty?*

Joseph: *As long as I don't fade away like a damp squib.*

Ava: *Not likely. There's nothing damp squib like about you. I've just tried to find a damp squib emoticon, but there isn't one so here's a squid instead. Gap in the market for you right there, tech nerd.*

Joseph: *That's it, I'm going to make my fortune designing a damp squib emoji.*

Ava: *As long as you call it Ava.*

Joseph: *Of course. I wouldn't want you coming after me for a cut of the profits. So, what's happening?*

Ava: *I'm sitting outside Finn's house while he's inside shagging some random girl.*

Joseph: *What? No way.*

Ava: *Yes, way. We broke up. Or he broke up with me. But either way it's over, and he's in there doing you know what, and I'm balling my eyes out.*

Joseph: *Aw, Ava don't cry. Do you want me to go around there and knock him out?*

Ava: *Maybe.*

Joseph: *Can it keep till next time I'm home?*

Ava: *Suppose it'll have to.*

Joseph: *Are you still crying?*

Ava: *No. Not really. Later, squid boy.*

Joseph: *Later.*

Ava started the engine and drove away, tears tripping her sorry face.

Chapter 4

Guilt just about cracked open Ava's heart every time she pulled into the grounds of the nursing home Maggie resided in. A stroke had left the formerly robust and seemingly unstoppable Maggie paralysed down one side. Caring for Maggie at home had been Ava's intention and greatest wish, but Maggie had other ideas. Before the stroke had rendered her frail and dependent, she had set the wheels in motion to gain admittance into the Sisters of Mercy convent nursing home.

Ava parked her car in the section marked out for visitors and walked up the crunchy gravel driveway. Quinn the gardener, who tended to keep to himself, gave her a cursory nod as she passed him on her way. The former converted convent building was set in sumptuously lush and landscaped grounds. The twelve-foot-high hot pink rhododendrons and bridal white azaleas in full bloom were enough to lift the weary spirits of the most depressed resident. The main building had been a large family home before being bought by the church many years earlier, to house the Sisters of Mercy nuns. In an effort to earn their keep, the Sisters of Mercy had turned their hands to managing a nursing home as a profitable enterprise, much to the Bishop's pleasure.

Ava buzzed the intercom and was waved in by Sister Lucy, a tall angular-looking day-nurse who reminded Ava of Miss Clavel from Ludwig Bemelman's Madeline books. She pushed open the heavy wood door and entered the warm hallway. Security was more about keeping the more senile residents in than visitors out.

Ava thought Sister Lucy suited her name. She was light and bright with a twinkle in her eye that suggested a certain mischief. There were still a few nuns working at the care home, though they were a dying breed. While most of the sisters working as carers were nice, some could be standoffish and preoccupied as if listening to some internal Godly dialogue. Sister Lucy was always clued in and seemed to be a buffer between the nuns and the outside world.

'Good afternoon, Ava. How are we finding you today?' Sister Lucy asked in her southern Irish brogue that always lifted Ava's mood and made her want to smile.

'Grand, Sister Lucy. Everyone okay here?' she asked in her tentative way of finding out if anyone had died overnight. Ava had come to realise that success rate for the carers and the sisters was to see their residents off comfortably to the next life. Not that there was any helping hand, so to speak. No, it was more a matter of feeling that their residents were moving on, and part of their job was to help prepare them to meet their next landlord with a clean conscience and a good reference.

'Maureen Harper was looking a bit peaky, but she seems to have picked up,' Sister Lucy replied all smiles as if to indicate, sure wasn't Maureen Harper the lucky one to be one step closer to the great shindig in the sky. 'Your gran slept well, and we managed to get the medication into her without a fight.'

Ava knew that Maggie resisted the tablets. She had a distrust of taking anything even remotely medicinal. To take a paracetamol to cure a headache was a sign of pure weakness in Maggie's book, and she considered anyone ridiculous enough to take vitamin supplements as needing their head seeing to.

Ava made her way down the hushed corridor to Maggie's room. She had to admit the carers had created a lovely homely feel. When Ava had initially thought of Maggie going into a nursing home, she imagined odours of boiled cabbage and fermenting wee, but the old convent house smelled of incense, melting candle wax and cinnamon, a churchy smell that seemed to come from the nuns themselves.

Just as Ava was about to turn into Maggie's room, she took a deep breath, as if to brace herself. Maggie was sat on her comfy chair, with her feet up on the coffee-coloured suede pouffe Ava had purchased for her. She was facing the window overlooking the gardens and turned her head as Ava walked in.

'Hi, Gran. How are you doing?' Ava was aware of her over-breezy tone. She couldn't help it. No matter how nice the carers were or how comfortable the home felt, she still struggled with a lump in her throat when she visited Maggie. To compensate for her rush of emotions, guilt mingled with sadness, she tried to sound all carefree and bright whenever she arrived. Always the same chirpy tone, which Ava knew rang out as forced and unnatural. She longed to go back to the days when Maggie was the carer, the responsible adult who made all the hard decisions, and protected Ava from the harsher side of life. Selfish as that was, she couldn't help but want to revert to their former safe and comfortable relationship.

Maggie looked up and tried to smile. One side of her mouth gamely cooperated.

'Ah, there you are,' she said as if she had expected Ava to appear at that exact minute. The stroke had affected her speech, but Ava could understand her well enough.

'The shop was busy today, Gran. Hazel took another standing order for that big hotel at the bottom of Royal Avenue. I made a lovely arrangement of those scented stocks you like with cream germini and blush pink roses with just a few touches of baby's breath spray. You would have loved it.' Ava tried to keep the conversation going, knowing that Maggie wasn't up to saying much.

'Aye,' Maggie managed, and waggled her head in an approximation of a nod of agreement while raising her good hand to point to the vase on the windowsill filled with lilac, pink and white lisianthus which Ava had brought in a couple of days before. Maggie's fingers were gnarled claws, mutated by arthritis and old age. Ava took a tissue from the bedside cabinet and wiped the spittle collecting in the corner of Maggie's sunken hole of a mouth. Without her false teeth to give her face form and structure, her whole mouth looked like it was turning in on itself, an empty cave of unsaid words.

'Shall I change the water for you; keep them fresh for a little bit longer?' Ava asked, not waiting for an answer and already busying herself with the flowers.

Ava tidied up the room a little. Moving the jug and the glass from the bedside table, straightening the already perfectly made bed and plumping up the starchy-covered pillows; she liked to pretend she was being useful and that she was still looking after Maggie. Her boggy, peat-coloured eyes were misted by age, but still held Ava's gaze with an intensity which time could not diminish.

For once, Ava had loads she wanted to say. She longed to pour her heart out about Finlay, call him all the bad names under the sun, and have Maggie tell her he wasn't worth crying over. Instead, she launched straight into the mystery home.

'Gran, I'm thinking of moving to a new house. Would you mind?' Ava emptied the murky, stagnant water from the jug which still held the pink and lilac but wilting lisianthus she had brought in a week earlier. The heating was always turned up too high in the rooms, so the flowers died quickly, a scummy mildew building up on the inside of the vase.

Maggie just stared ahead, watching the gardener, through the window, manoeuvre his sit-on lawnmower over the flat stretch of lawn.

'I'm not thinking of selling Moonstone Street, it's your home after all. But something so strange has happened, Gran. I've inherited a house. A lovely, big, old house. Nothing this exciting has ever happened to me before, Gran, and I just want to run with this and see where I end up. Do you know what I mean?'

Ava was aware she was rambling, but Maggie's lack of response made Ava want to fill up the silences. She turned the tap off and replaced the jug on the bedside cabinet with a fresh bunch of lime-green hydrangea and pink curcuma.

Since seeing Finlay with that girl, Ava had been convinced she was doing the right thing. Life was supposed to be about growing, experiencing new things, moving onwards, but all Ava had been doing, for the last God knows how many years, was waiting time out. Letting life drift past her instead of rushing headlong into it.

She had spent the previous night torturing herself, visualising her life ten years, twenty years, from now, and the only picture she could foresee was one where she was sitting in the floral green patterned armchair in Moonstone Street watching wildlife documentaries with only Chris Packham for company. No harm to Chris Packham but she needed something more than conversation about nesting and sibling owls eating each other to keep her warm at night.

Number ninety-seven was an opportunity to be grasped. She didn't know what it would bring, but surely something different, something more, was better than what she had at present.

She sat down close to Maggie, their knees touching. Maggie was wearing the navy trousers Ava had bought for her from Marks and Spencer with a nylon cream blouse buttoned up to her scrawny, tortoise-like neck. One of the nursing attendants would have washed and dressed her that morning. It was a Sunday, so they always tried to dress everyone in their good clothes.

Maggie was smiling her crooked, lopsided smile and with her good hand, she tried to reach over to pat Ava's knee. It was as close as Ava was going to get to a sign of approval.

'You used to dance everywhere. Those feet never sat still; dum de, dum de dum, I'd hum and off you'd go. Took you to Maria Black's the Irish dancing class up the Ravenhill Road, do you recall?'

'Of course, I remember.' Ava was used to this. Sometimes, Maggie would go off reminiscing, seemingly oblivious to the conversation they were having.

'The costume cost me a right few bob even though I bought it second-hand off Bridie McLetham. You swirled around and around in it, the full skirt floating out with your every turn. It was royal blue with beautiful swirls of coloured interlinking embroidered chains. A cape sat on your shoulders held on by two brooches I found down in Smithfield market.'

Ava smiled. Maggie's face was alight with the memories. She was off on one. There would be no stopping her now; one story after the other would fill their conversation. Ava would be lucky to get a word in edgeways as Maggie would travel into the past.

'Do you remember your wee rag doll? That wee cloth thing was threadbare by the time I threw it out. Holly Hobbie was her name and you carried it everywhere. Cried for days over that doll, you did. But sure, what was the point of keeping it when it was worn out? I wasn't one for holding onto things for the sake of it.

'Your granddad used to walk you along the Lagan. I used to say to him, go slow now she's only a youngster, but he said you would skip along no bother, never complained or wanted carrying. If you did get too tired he would put you up on his shoulders. 'Up in the sky' you called it. You were the light of our world. Once Scarlett went, we looked to you to fill the void, and God knows you helped to mend my broken heart. Was it you or was it Scarlett he walked along the Lagan? I can't remember. It's all mixed up now.'

Since the second stroke, Maggie had really struggled. She seemed so frail and vulnerable, but Ava knew she was being well looked after. She could always give up work and spend her days looking after Maggie, but then she knew it wasn't what Maggie wanted and besides, Ava wouldn't be able to afford to hold onto Mount Pleasant Square with no salary coming in. Not that what she earned was a great deal. Still, she couldn't complain since money had never been a priority before and now for the first time in her life she was working out how to maximise her income while cutting back on her unnecessary expenditure — all with the intention of ploughing every spare penny into Mount Pleasant Square. Just the bare essential maintenance work to make the house decent enough to live in was scarily expensive. She had toyed with the idea of taking in lodgers, but the thought of sharing with strangers was a step too far out of her comfort zone.

The plumber had told her that the whole heating system needed to be ripped out. She was pretty sure the house needed rewiring, and that would run into thousands of pounds before she even began thinking of the kitchen and bathroom remodelling. It was a crying shame that she did not have Finlay's expertise on hand. Maybe it was worth giving him a call to give the house a once-over in a professional capacity.

In the wee lonely hours of the night, she wondered was she really being naive to take on the house. She had a romanticised view of scrubbing down skirting boards and unearthing original 1900s features, but in her heart, she knew it would be a hard slog just to make the house semi-habitable.

When she thought of the light coming in through the stained-glass window and the old cast iron bath, though it was stained a horrible shade of ochre, the wonderful view of the garden from the back bedroom and the quirky little walk-in cupboard which would have served as a pantry, she knew it would be worth all the hard work and expense.

Somebody wanted her to have the house, and it felt right to try to make a go of it. Maybe Maggie's health would improve, and Ava could make the house comfortable enough to bring her home. In the meantime, she had a lot of work to do. Hazel was heading off on her romantic trip to Sorrento, so Ava was to be left in charge of the shop.

She had to sort out some finances to start the repairs on the house and she intended to make an appointment with that solicitor Amanda again, to try to find out the identity of her benefactor and ask her how she could go looking for her mother. She had done a search on Niamh's computer in the vain hope that modern technology would lead her straight to her mother. She had typed "Scarlett Connors" into Google waiting to see what it would throw out at her. But all they could find were references to her music days. There was nothing to give them a clue as to what she was doing now or where she was living.

Maggie's failing health had kick-started a whole range of emotions in Ava; most significantly, she couldn't stop thinking about her mum. She was curious for the first time in her life. What was she like? Did she not care enough about Ava to check in on her from time to time? Try as she had to push such thoughts from her head, she had been unsettled by finishing with Finlay and the inheritance of Mount Pleasant Square. Something had shifted in her and for once she felt brave enough to go with it. Finding Scarlett, or at least finding out what had become of her, seemed important.

Perhaps Ava was getting old, nearly thirty and not yet settled down, and then thinking of Mount Pleasant Square too, it made her want to be part of a family. A proper family.

Every now and then over the years she had thought about tracking down her mum. But as she became older, she didn't want to ask Maggie for fear of upsetting her. She assumed that Scarlett and Maggie had fought and that the rift had been beyond healing.

Sometimes when she was growing up she would daydream about Scarlett coming back for her. They would hug and kiss and make everything just perfect and be the best mother daughter team ever. She imagined Scarlett looking like Doris Day, all puffed up coiffured blonde hair and little matchy-matchy suits, shoes and a clutch bag. She would march right on in and they would all live happily in Moonstone Street.

But deep down, Ava knew that Maggie had been good to her and was all she could ever wish for. For whatever reason, Scarlett couldn't give her the security and love Maggie had lavished on her, and Ava would never forget that.

The door opened, and a nursing attendant popped her head round.

'Tea for you?' she asked in a voice still heavy with her Filipino accent.

'Yes please, Nena.' Ava accepted the two cups of tea and helped herself to the tea trolley biscuits when it was rolled in.

'I will help you feed Mrs Connors. She looks good today. I gave her lunch and she ate all of it.' Her dark eyes radiated compassion.

'I'll manage, thanks. You go and have a cup of tea yourself,' Ava said as she set about helping Maggie sip the lukewarm tea. Like any small task of helping Maggie, Ava enjoyed doing it.

'Oh, I'm too busy for tea. Everyone is waiting for their supper.' Nena laughed, not complaining at all, seemingly happy to be needed.

Ava was touched by Nena's gentle kindness. Nothing ever seemed to be too much trouble for her. Ava wondered who she had left behind in the Philippines to come to Belfast to seek work. Maybe she had left a baby girl in the hands of her mother, just like Scarlett had done.

Nothing was ever black and white. Everyone had their reasons.

Hey Joseph. Saw your Facebook post. Looked amazing.

One of those nights. They throw these mad parties, and everyone gets roaring drunk, but if you've any sense you stay sober enough to know your boss is watching.

Hope you behaved.

Of course. I'm always well behaved. How's Maggie?

She's having a snooze. I'm at the care home now.

Hope you are okay, too.

Yeah, sorry about the other night. I'm pathetic.

Didn't like to say. You know he doesn't deserve you.

According to Niamh, I didn't deserve him.

What does Niamh know about anything?

Quite a lot. She's the one with all the relationship experience.

And look where that gets her! Up shit creek without a paddle.

True. Here, I have to go. Talk soon.

Yeah, soon.

Chapter 5

L ater that night, Ava embarked on the clear-out. It had been hanging over her for weeks like an opportunistic migraine waiting to pounce. She knew that if she was going to move out, it would be sensible to de-clutter and sort things out in advance. There was no point putting it off, and she knew that as soon as she started work on number ninety-seven, she would be so consumed by it, that she would rarely have time to check in on Moonstone Street, let alone tidy it up.

She decided to get stuck in upstairs and work her way down. She climbed the steep, narrow staircase suddenly feeling energised. If she was actually sorting out Moonstone Street, then moving into number ninety-seven seemed more real. It was no longer a dream or a far-off plan to be contemplated and looked forward to. It was actually going to happen.

Maggie's house may have been small, but she had accumulated five decades' worth of living, all packed in drawers, cupboards and boxes stacked on top of the wardrobes. Most of it was old faded newspapers, the reason they were kept long forgotten, some of Ava's school books and school reports, even old Irish dancing medals and programmes listing the reels and the jigs and naming the contenders. Junk really, but it could take up to a month to sort through and separate the stuff worth keeping from that which needed to be dumped.

Ava had no intention of spending weeks trawling through it all. She wasn't going to be sentimental about it. It was a clear-out job that needed to be done with a ruthless heart, not weighed down by maudlin thoughts dressed up as memories. Maggie had intended to do it for years but as always, she gave up at the thought of chucking out things she had long forgotten why she had kept in the first place. Ava could do a better job since she didn't intend to pore over every photo or run through the story related to each ornament or novelty item. She would be clinical and cold and just get on with it. Besides, it would be so much easier to do while Maggie was still alive. The thought of clearing out the house after Maggie's death would have seemed too final and emotional, at least now it was a work in progress, not an expurgation of their life.

Ava started with a large cardboard box with Fyffes bananas printed across it in a faded royal blue print. The box had stayed on top of the wardrobe in Maggie's room for so long that it had ceased to be noticed. Ava stood on the bed and reached up to lift the large box down. A cloud of dust made her cough, but undeterred she opened a black plastic bin bag in preparation for the rubbish to be discarded.

Ava rummaged through the sediment of Maggie's life, the bits and pieces which had sunk to the lowly depths of her awareness and sat decaying and gathering dust for years.

The sorting was almost fun. Ava picked up objects like an old porcelain shepherdess ornament that she remembered sitting on the windowsill for years, until it had been knocked down and cracked. Instead of throwing it out, for some reason, Maggie had kept it until it had been forgotten. There was an old brass compass which Ava thought had probably belonged to her grandfather, Paddy. She put it to one side, not wanting to part with it, and then reprimanded herself, thinking if she decided to keep every little object of interest she would get nowhere. The hours went by, and by the time she had three oversized bags full of rubbish and two earmarked for the Cancer Research shop, she felt that she had made good headway.

Ava decided to take a break and went back downstairs to make a cup of tea. There was one box, an old leatherette cutlery canteen, she had set aside without going through, knowing it contained mementoes of her mother, photographs and newspaper clippings, and thought she would sit back on Maggie's bed with her cup of tea and have a poke through it.

Ava had vague memories of looking through the container years earlier with Maggie. They had stored photographs in it and a few postcards Scarlett had sent from her travels, but over the years the box had been pushed to the back of the wardrobe, and to the back of their minds.

Setting her mug of strong tea on the bedside cabinet, she sat on Maggie's pale blue candlewick-covered bed ready to reminisce and reconnect with the few memories she had of Scarlett. Ava coughed as a scratchy dryness caught in her throat. Dust floated around her like a mist of time. Everything she touched seemed to have a layer of years' worth of dust accumulating as if to prove just how long the boxes and possessions had gone unnoticed.

She pulled a pillow behind her back and made herself comfortable to sort through the contents. She opened the tarnished gold-coloured catch on the old royal-blue leatherette box and found amongst the silver-grey satin-lined box, with grooves shaped to hold the long-since-vanished cutlery, the pages of a letter carefully folded over and addressed to Ava in Maggie's scrawling hand writing. The writing was not quite as bad as it had become in the months before she went into the Sisters of Mercy home. Her letters were looping and sloping forward as if in haste to finish what needed to be said.

Ava, if you are reading this, then one of two things has happened—either I am dead and sleeping with the angels in heaven, God rest my soul, or you have been looking through stuff you have no right to be searching through. If it's the latter, fold this letter up at once, child, and we will speak no more about it.

Ava inhaled sharply. Letter writing from the grave wasn't Maggie's style. Ava shivered, thinking of her grandmother sitting at their little kitchen table with the red and white gingham tablecloth, to compose a letter she intended to be read when she was dead. Ava couldn't resist reading on, despite Maggie's express instruction.

Right, I assume I am dead. I hope you gave me a good send off. I better have been laid out in the good navy suit I bought in the Country Casuals sale. The woman in the shop said the pink scarf lifted my colouring so I draped it over the suit hanger hoping you would have the sense to put it on me for my wake.

I always kept it at the front of the wardrobe to make sure you noticed it when you would be looking for something to dress me in. I hope you used O'Mallie's funeral directors. The other crowd have a reputation for not doing the hair and make-up to a good enough standard, and I would like to look my best, not like poor Nessie Hamill who was no more like herself than my left leg is like a sparrow's beak.

I wonder who came. Did you serve the tea in my good Royal Doulton tableware? The cake stand is a bit wonky but hopefully it did the job, providing the cakes were light and fluffy the way I bake them. If you bought them in from McKearney's bakery they will be as hard as the calluses on a farmer's hands.

Sorry I am digressing. I am avoiding the issue as ever. I may have made some mistakes in my life but you should know they were done in the name of love, love for you.

Anyways. The purpose of this letter is to fill you in, so to speak. I wasn't one for dwelling on the past, as you know, and I let things go by without explaining them to you. You were always such a good girl and never gave me a moment's bother, except for that time you stayed out late and drank that snakebite concoction. I hope you learnt your lesson — never mix blackcurrant Ribena with lemonade, the bubbles do something to the syrup and it can make you light-headed.

Perhaps I should start at the beginning. They say it's all in the name and maybe that was part of the problem. I couldn't see past the name Scarlett. Thought it was the most beautiful name ever and when Rhett Butler took Scarlett in his arms I just about swooned in the back row of the stalls of the New Vic. So, you see, when my baby came along I wanted to name her Scarlett, hoping for a feisty beauty, but I got more than I bargained for.

I should have listened to the priest, they are nearly always right. Father Gilligan did the baptism rites and when he asked for the name and I said, 'Scarlett' loud and proud for all to hear, he muttered something about pagan names and bad seeds and christened her Mary instead. I didn't give a hoot. So, what if she was Mary on her baptism form? When we went down to the City Hall to register the birth, your granddad told the official his daughter was to be named Scarlett Mary Connors. I thought my heart would burst with pride at him standing up for the name I wanted for that bonny weeun with the head of dark hair.

As my luck would have it, the priest was right. Scarlett lived up to her name and became the feisty beauty I'd hoped for. Of course, I hadn't thought of how raising a girl with a temperament and a wilful streak to frighten the gypsies would be so hard. Her antics near enough killed your poor granddad, God rest his soul in Heaven with the angels and saints.

Our Scarlett grew up to have raven black hair, eyes the colour of violets and skin as clear and luminous as the moon. A real beauty, they all said so, even the Connor's cousins couldn't deny our Scarlett had more than her fair share of looks, and it near enough choked your great aunt Sadie Connors to admit it. Of course, Grandma Connors said it would be her curse, and maybe she was proved right in the end. Too good-looking for her own good, she had said.

It was like having a peep into the history of her life, seeing it from Maggie's perspective for the first time and realising the loss she must have felt when Scarlett moved away. Tucked behind the letter, Ava found a bundle of photographs. They were little four by four squares of faded colour photos, each holding an image of Scarlett. In one of them she was standing proud wearing a full-length white broderie Anglaise first communion dress, her hands clasped piously in prayer with pearl rosary beads entwined around her little fingers. Her long, dark hair covered in a soft, white veil secured by a plastic comb topped with fabric roses.

Another showed her looking awkwardly from beneath a wide-brimmed straw hat, sitting on a beach, her hair blowing behind her. She looked about fourteen, her eyes avoiding the camera and her mouth contorted into a huffy little pout, seemingly unhappy to be dragged along for a day at the seaside let alone to be photographed.

Ava recognised the next image. It was a photograph she had seen before, Scarlett wearing tight jeans with a T-shirt and a denim jacket draped over her shoulders with an acoustic guitar resting against her legs as if it were a casual prop.

A fourth photograph showed a young Scarlett sat between her mother and father on a sofa in what looked like Grandma Connors' house. She was wearing a gingham shirt, the collar a huge wide lapelled creation that made Ava smile. Her bare knees stuck out from beneath her skirt and she had russet-coloured boots on which rose up to just below her knees. Maggie and Paddy were sitting as if sandwiching Scarlett in, looking like they were trying to force her to stay with them.

And then Ava found one of Scarlett photographed close up: wide eyed and smiling with Ava as a baby resting on her shoulder. Her blue-black lustrous hair draped like a silk scarf around her pale face. Ava felt her heart lurch. It was an image of such tenderness and love that she felt certain her mother had loved her. Scarlett hadn't just run off without it impacting on her too. What had it cost the young girl in the photograph to leave behind the child snuggled contently into her neck?

Amongst the keepsakes on top of the wardrobe, Ava found a scrapbook full of old newspaper clippings about Scarlett's success in the States. The Belfast Telegraph carried a full-length photo of her holding her album cover, looking serious. Her band stood behind her as if to emphasise that Scarlett was the main attraction. The headline read, 'Local girl tops the hit parade'. Other clippings were album reviews, small pieces about how well she was doing Stateside. The clippings stopped at 1979, the year after Ava was born. Several pages of the scrapbook lay unfilled as if waiting for someone to pick up the thread of the story and fill them in.

Ava went back to reading the letter, feeling that she was unravelling her own past, along with her mother's, her heart contracting and beating as always but now filled with a renewed yearning to know more.

Ava felt as if everything and yet nothing had changed. The kaleidoscope of her soul had shifted ever so slightly, rearranging everything she believed and revealing a whole new picture.

Chapter 6

'Operation recovery is underway,' said Niamh, teasing Ava's hair into a low chignon. They had abandoned the loose topknot and rejected the quiff fringe.

'What exactly are you supposed to be recovering?' asked Ava, eyeing her reflection in the mirror with something approaching concern.

'Your dignity, your looks,' replied Niamh as she looked in the mirror at her creation with a critical eye.

'Your *man*,' piped up Cal who was busy trying to sort out Niamh's jewellery kit. He was stood holding a tumble of necklaces all entwined in a mess of glittery gold and silver.

'Girl, you are one lazy cow. Would you look at the state of these,' he said holding up the knotted chains and beads for them to see.

Ava tried to pull away from Niamh's grasp as a shower of hairspray rained down on her head, inducing a fifty-a-day type coughing fit.

'No one mentioned *recovering Finlay*. Besides, he doesn't seem to want to be recovered,' said Ava as Niamh pulled on her hair a bit too harshly for her liking. 'Oi, go easy.'

Cal rolled his eyes in mock exasperation. 'Honey child, do you know nothing? The first thing a man does to win his woman back is make her jealous. That wee set-up was all for your benefit.'

'I wish I had your confidence, Cal, but I don't think I was on his mind when those curtains closed.' Ava sighed, then took a hefty swig of her wine to dull the aching pain of the memory.

'Listen, I know a thing or two about men. Sure, haven't I been round the block and up the entry a few times more than you, and when a man feels snubbed he does what comes naturally and grabs another bit, to help ease him over the heartache. Tis the way of the world,' Cal said sagely, as if he knew only too well how the machinations of the male mind worked.

'He is right, you know,' Niamh replied, helping herself to more wine. 'Cal has more experience than both of us put together. He's been round the block and up the entry many a Friday night. If Finlay wanted you back the first thing he would do would be to put out and about his manhood, knowing full well in this town you'd get wind of it.'

'I think you two are forgetting Finlay is not the hard-done-by party here. He dropped me, so why would he be looking to make me jealous?' asked Ava reasonably.

'Girl-child, yer man wanted to feel loved, appreciated, and you and your frigid fandanny had frozen him out. So, he does the only thing *to do* and tells you it's over. That doesn't mean he wants it to *be over*, he just wants to make you want him more,' said Cal while checking out his reflection in the mirror and adjusting his spiked hair.

'And we, Ava Connors, are going to help you find your inner sex kitten, starting with a new look and a night out to blow your socks off,' Niamh said smiling.

'Once you are in the zone of sexed up honeyness, he'll come running back like a dog with two dicks,' concluded Cal.

'What am I doing, letting you two take charge of my love life?' groaned Ava, putting her head in her hands.

Niamh put her hand on Ava's shoulder and looked at her in the reflection of the mirror. 'Doris Day, I hate to spell it out to you, but you ain't got a love life. That's why your fairy godmothers are here. Trust us we're the lurve doctors. Here to cure your every ill.'

Ava had a feeling she might regret it but hell, what else had she to do on a Saturday night?

*

Ava woke out of a heavy sleep and was aware of a scratchy dryness at the back of her throat. Her tongue felt rough and parched like a piece of old shammy leather left to gather dust in a long-forgotten kitchen drawer. A desperate stiffness seemed to spread outwards down her jaw, around her neck and shoulders and finally became a searing pain crashing through her head. She tried to move but it was as if her body had been submerged in concrete, cold and solid, holding her down.

Where am I? She thought as another burst of pain radiated at her temples. *Maybe I've been drugged and left for dead with one of my kidneys stolen and put for sale on eBay.* But the pain centred in her head and her raspy, starchy mouth tasted of soured wine, indicating that her suffering was most likely to be all self-inflicted. It had been so long since she had experienced a hangover that she had forgotten how awful it could be.

She heard a low guttural groan and then realised it was coming from herself. Jagged shards of memory punctuated her consciousness as she recalled the previous night. She could remember drinking shots, amber and verdant-coloured drinks with names like Moon Beam, Siren, and Bomber. There was music, loud and thumping, and lights. Raucous laughter and some carry on with throwing back shots like there was no tomorrow.

A flash of seeing someone who vaguely looked like Ava dancing on a stage and doing a seductive striptease came into her mind. It was like an out-of-body experience where she could see what she was doing yet had no control to stop herself. *Oh no*, she groaned inwardly, *I can't have.*

But she had, and now remembering, in the cold light of day, she was surprised to find herself smiling, and then silently giggling as she recalled the silly dance she had done with a huge fluffy pink ostrich feather between her legs.

Niamh and Cal had taken her to The Kitty House, a club with a burlesque theme night in full throw. They had an open mike segment where members of the audience were invited up on stage to help Betty Boom Boom do her thing. Cal had practically dragged Ava up to the stage and then, when the spotlight fell on her and the audience had cheered, she found herself complying and being rushed to the wings where she was trussed up in a red satin basque with black glittery fringing and high black patent boots which were a couple of sizes too big. She could remember saying that she looked like a drag queen and someone else saying she should be so lucky.

Suddenly she was led out onto the stage by Betty who whispered into her ear in a broad west Belfast accent, 'you look great, just copy me.' Before she knew it, she was swinging her hips slowly to the jazzy soundtrack and sucking her tummy in, while trying to stick her ass out and rotate it in time to the music. The bright stage lights dazzled her, preventing her from seeing the audience, but she was acutely aware of them shouting encouragement and spurring her on.

They had clapped appreciatively. Someone wolf whistled. It wasn't seedy or full of dirty old men. The crowd were mainly office workers, and a hen party, young people out for entertainment and a night of laughs. Ava had never felt such a surge of sparky energy before. She felt lit-up from her toes to the ends of her hair. Everything felt electric and alive. At one point, she'd taken a selfie and sent it to Joseph.

Afterwards, Ava, Niamh and Cal had screeched with laughter and recounted the scene with Cal giving a full-on rendition in the middle of Shaftesbury Square with the same ostrich feather sticking out from between his bare bum cheeks as he dropped his trousers for the hell of it.

Beyond that, Ava could not remember making it home. Come to think of it, this didn't feel like her bed. She turned over, in spite of the dull headache threatening to explode into a fierce furnace of pain, and there right beside her in the bed was something or someone warm and solid.

Please God, let me be in Niamh's bed with her and not Cal or some poor hapless fella I've accidentally picked up at the club, Ava thought with terror.

Tentatively she opened one eye, the other was glued solid and wouldn't budge. She could make out the smooth, muscular back which told her instantly that her bed companion was neither Niamh nor the delicately built Cal.

Think, think, think. Who did she meet last night? Had she run into Finlay and kissed and made up? No, she would have remembered, and besides, she was sure this wasn't Finlay's bedroom or his back she was looking at with her one good eye. She tried to cast a glance around the room to find some clue as to where she was. The pillow was soft and the bed felt solid, comfortable and luxurious so at least she hadn't woken up in some student dive.

The curtains were closed but seemed to be some sort of silvery voile material, thin enough to let some light through to enable her to see around. The early morning sunlight had cast a soothing creamy yellow glow on the walls and she could just about see a tall set of drawers which were covered in bottles of hair products, aftershave and cologne. On the wooden oak floor, over in the corner, she could make out a television and gaming console which was sat next to a pile of dirty clothes, jeans and T-shirts and her own strappy sandals.

Then whoever was beside her groaned and moved. Ava ducked her head under the duvet, desperate to hide and put off the inevitable moment, when she would have to face whoever had hauled her home with them. She was sure she hadn't jumped on the first fella she had seen. It wasn't her style to pick up random strangers. God, she could have been raped or murdered. Shame and embarrassment made her flush crimson red. Maybe he had spiked her drink and had taken advantage of her.

She felt a warm hand reach down for her breast and give it a playful squeeze. *Shit, I'm naked,* she thought as his fingers stroked her, making her nipples stiffen involuntarily.

'Come here, you,' he said, his voice rough and sexy, thick with sleep, as he wriggled under the duvet to be close to her.

And then she remembered: hard, passionate kisses, deep tongues and grasping hands roaming all over her body as she yanked at his zipper and pulled him out into her eager hand.

Ava thought she was going to black out from the shock of what she had just remembered. She was in bed, naked, having done the dirty deed with none other than Ben Dale, her boss's son.

Chapter 7

Ava studied her face in the mirror, trying to detect a change. Somehow, between finishing with Finlay and deciding to move into number ninety-seven, she felt that her whole life was in a state of flux and that she must surely be visibly different. She could barely believe that she had participated in a wild night out which had culminated in sex with Ben.

To say it was out of character was an understatement. Ava Connors played it safe. She didn't do wild one-night stands and she could count on one hand the number of boys she had kissed. It was as if she had taken leave of her senses.

But no, she couldn't deny that the same girl who had played it safe all her life, the one with the sweetheart-shaped face looking back at her, was the one who had shifted her boss's son. God, the mortification of it. Any time she had met him in the shop he had been courteous and nice but was most definitely too young for her. How could she ever look him in the eye over the pots of peonies again?

She dragged a hand through her straggly, turf-brown hair and rubbed at her sorrowful eyes, feeling the remains of dried mascara crumbling under her fingertips. All that warpaint and look where it got her. Cal had plucked and shaped her eyebrows into perfect arches that lifted her face and made her seem slightly surprised, and shaded and highlighted her previously non-existent cheekbones, but ultimately, the operation recovery makeover had ended in disaster.

In the cold light of day, she was left looking at the original Ava Connors. Boring, predictable Ava. Ava who had never done anything out of the ordinary in her life before. Who went to work every day, visited her poor sick grandmother, and returned to her ordinary little house to watch predictable soap operas and read crime novels while nibbling on bars of Galaxy chocolate and drinking tonic water — without the gin. She was the first to admit it — she was plain boring. Dull as drizzle.

But then she smiled, remembering Ben's thick muscular legs, the feel of his smooth torso and the gentleness of his touch on her skin. She felt flushed just thinking about him. The long lingering, beer-tasting kisses and the smell of his skin, damp with a musky sweat.

If someone had told her she would end up sleeping with Hazel's — her friend and boss — twenty-year-old son, Ava would have balked at the idea, gagged even. Ben may have been big, beautiful and blonde, but he was oh so wrong for her. For starters, he was twenty. *Twenty*, for God's sake. What had she been thinking? Not a lot beyond being shagged senseless, if she were honest. The alcohol combined with a night of watching Betty Boom Boom do her stuff with the Velvet Vixens in the Kitty House had awakened something in Ava which she didn't know existed.

And then there was the whole issue of working for his mother who thought the sun shone out of his peachy cute ass and hated every girlfriend he ever brought home. Not that Ava was under any illusions of being brought home to meet the parents. She cringed as she thought of how Hazel would sometimes call him Benji, pinching his cheeks like he was an errant schoolboy. If only Hazel knew what a bad boy he really was. But stop, Ava thought, she couldn't even allow herself the luxury of enjoying the memory. The night had come back to her in random scenes: ear nibbling, shared drinks in some dark corner of a bar, giggling while he kissed her neck and then later pleasuring each other in that big soft bed. In other words, behaving badly. Very badly.

Again, Ava reprimanded herself for acting so out of character.

It wasn't that Ben wasn't good looking, funny and kind, but he still lived at home, a home he treated like a hotel according to his often-exasperated mother and while he had elements of the mammy's boy about him, he led a boy-about-town existence in hot pursuit of a good time fuelled by women and beer. Okay, so Ava wasn't so quick to have flown the family nest herself, but sure girls could get away with it more so than boys, she reasoned, all too aware of how sexist that was.

She had accepted his offer of breakfast and while he was putting it together she excused herself and went to the bathroom to pee and freshen up. With her hair dragged into a hasty ponytail, courtesy of an elastic band nicked from Hazel's Clarins-Dermologica-and-Aveda-cluttered bathroom shelf, Ava went back downstairs intending to call a taxi. It would cost a small fortune to get from Crawfordsburn to home, but she didn't want to expect Ben to give her a lift. She didn't need to be in an enclosed space, watching him and blushing at the thought of what they might have done the night before.

'Hey, where are you rushing off to?' he asked in his slow, sexy voice, taking her into his arms as she came down the stairs. He had a way of filling up the room just with his presence, no mean feat since Hazel's hallway was near enough the size of the whole of the little house on Moonstone Street.

'I'm off home. Thanks for a great night, Ben. I mean it, from what I can remember it was a great night but please, your mum can't ever know about this.' Ava was pleading as she looked up into his eyes which she noticed for the first time were sea green with flecks of vibrant amber.

'Hey, I'm a big boy. So what if we're going out together. Mum won't mind she loves you,' he said, his eyes wide and innocent.

'Be real, will you, Ben, you're twenty and I'm… I'm too old to be going out with you. We had a nice night together. Let's leave it at that and keep it to ourselves.'

'Yo, bro. Hiya, Ava.'

They both turned, Ben's arms still wrapped around Ava, as Daniel came padding down the stairs with his hand shoved down his boxer shorts, scratching his balls.

'You two kept me awake half the night. Like a pack of dogs on heat.' He laughed to himself as he sloped off to Hazel's interior-designed kitchen.

'I think I'm going to be sick,' Ava groaned before rushing off to the downstairs bathroom. She could never allow this to happen again. It was so out of character. What was happening to her?

*

Niamh had howled with laughter, the evening after, when Ava recounted wakening up beside Ben, in his mother's luxurious house overlooking the Lough.

'Ava, there was no prising the pair of you apart. You were at each other like your lives depended on it,' Niamh said, flicking a cigarette into a makeshift ashtray of a saucer while sitting in the living room of the house on Moonstone Street.

Ava told her how they had had a breakfast of croissants, fresh fruit and coffee thanks to the well-stocked cupboards Hazel had left before going to Sorrento with Robert.

Ben had been the perfect gentleman; asking Ava could he get her anything, was she feeling okay, after she had puked her guts up and wiped her face with the Cath Kidston towel. He acted like it was perfectly normal for the two of them to be sharing breakfast, following a night of drunken debauchery.

In fact, if anything, Ben was the one acting mature and grown-up. It was Ava who was shuddering at the flashback memories popping into her heavy head, like she was a teenager caught doing something she shouldn't. Knowing Ben's reputation as she did, thanks to Hazel's frequent recounting, he had more experience of this sort of thing. He would have woken up in countless beds following one-night stands and thought nothing of making conversation the morning after the steamy and heavy night before. Whereas Ava, the normally dowdy, timid and meek Ava, was painfully new to this.

She blamed Maggie; Ava had led such a sheltered life that when it came to men she was as green as a shot of Night Nurse. Ava had grown up to do what was expected of her. She didn't stay out all night like Niamh so often did, and even when she did find a boyfriend it was the respectable Finlay with his nice manners and clean-cut ways.

It was like discovering a fundamental gap in her education; she just didn't know how to behave *badly* and then deal with it the next day.

'How on earth am I going to face Hazel in the shop next week? I wish we had never gone to that student bar on Eglantine Avenue and then we wouldn't have run into him and none of this mess would have happened.' Ava groaned, burying her face in Maggie's best floral tapestry cushion.

'Calm yourself. Ben is hardly going to tell her so why should you mention it?' Niamh reasoned.

Ava lifted her face away from the cushion. 'Yeah, I suppose you're right. Hazel doesn't need to know. Maybe I can just pretend it never happened and put it down to a night of too much drink and bad company.'

'Listen, honey, you were the one dancing on a stage with tassels and a feather boa and then jumping the bones of the sumptuous Ben,' Niamh said, acting all indignant at being referred to as bad company. 'Sure, we had a great time, didn't we?'

Ava smiled; she couldn't help herself. 'The best!'

But really, when she thought about it, to have fallen into bed with Ben was the height of ridiculousness. How could she face Hazel over the bunches of pussy willows and hollyhocks without dying a thousand deaths of red-faced shame?

Despite all her protestations though, Ava had to admit, to herself and herself alone, that Ben Dale had something. There was something in the way he looked at her, in the way he said her name and let his fingers brush a stray croissant crumb from her mouth, lingering for just a second too long for it to be merely helpful, that unsettled her. He may have been playing a set routine, how to seduce in three simple steps, but Ava was frightened she was in danger of falling for it. Yet, she felt she shouldn't be held responsible for any lapse in judgement – it simply wasn't her fault that she was so unused to the wily ways of men like Ben.

*

After Niamh had gone home and Ava had cleared away the saucer full of cigarette butts, she lit a Dunnes Stores honeysuckle-scented candle to disperse the smell of smoke, before curling up on the sofa to reread Maggie's letter.

The clear-out had proved to be therapeutic in more ways than one. Ava had felt different reading those words, as if she was unearthing something deep within herself.

Maggie deciding to sign herself into the nursing home had been a huge adjustment for Ava. For the first time in her life, Ava was living alone. Finlay moving on had affected her deeply too. She was unsettled and uneasy. Life seemed so precarious, full of uncertainties, but there was a tiny sense of excitement in knowing that it was not necessarily mapped out after all.

She could admit to herself that Maggie's letter and the scrapbook full of memorabilia had fulfilled a sense of identity that Ava had longed for without even really knowing it. By the soft glow of candlelight, she read Maggie's words again.

I learnt from my mistake. When you came along with the gift tag of Ruby, I thought that name could spell trouble and I would be living your mother's teenage years all over again. So, we decided to call you Ava, your second name, which your mother chose out of respect for your great grandmother, a holy and good woman if ever there was one. As you probably know, Ruby Ava are the names on your birth certificate but as I'm sure you will agree you are much more of an Ava than a Ruby. Your mother tried to stick with Ruby but we soon wore her down and besides, later she couldn't really complain too much when she had taken herself off, but more of that later.

Anyway, I am getting off the point again. Your mother, the aptly named Scarlett, felt she was too big for a wee town like Belfast. She couldn't wait to take herself off to the bright lights of London.

She had a lovely voice. Oh, you should have heard her singing "Carrickfergus", it made the hairs on the back of your neck stand to attention. So, she set her sights on making a living singing in clubs in London. But our Scarlett wasn't satisfied with smoky nightclubs and a bartender's tips, so she thought America was where it was at. She had gone to London with some fella, a boyfriend if you will, long hair and a tattoo of a swan, and the two of them thought they could make it in LA. And they did by all accounts. Johnny was his name. Came from here so I was happy enough that he would look out for her.

When she went to America, we had the odd letter, full of herself, your granddad said, telling us all about her wonderful apartment on the beachfront, the great people she was mixing with, artists, actors and musicians and the like.

She was gone for almost two years when one day, out of the blue like, she turns up on the doorstep — I'd only just finished scrubbing it too — when this black taxi pulls up, and out she comes, larger than life, looking a bit tired and run down, I have to say. The taxi man took the suitcase out of the boot and left it at her feet, red suede platform boots they were too, distracted me for a moment I must say, for it took a second for me to realise that our Scarlett was right there in front of me and in her arms, she had a wee bundle. I near enough dropped to my knees on the spot.

Scarlett home, and with a baby. It was too much to take in. Anyways, I hurried her in off the doorstep before the neighbours clocked her, paid the taxi man, and put the kettle on.

I could hardly speak for the excitement of having her home, weeun an all.

I wasn't going to start on her. She looked done in to tell the truth, so I thought, 'Take it easy, Maggie.' I knew she had probably had a long flight and she looked wrecked. Pale and thin, so thin despite having had a baby just a month or so previous.

The baby was as good as gold, just lay there looking as content as anything with her eyes taking the place in. I put the pair of them to bed after giving Scarlett a good feed of eggs and bacon with a bit of soda bread fried in the pan, just the way she liked it.

We made a makeshift cot for the baby out of a drawer and a couple of blankets. God, you looked like a wee doll lying there in all snug and cosied-up.

When your granddad got in from work, he had many a question. Where had she been? Why hadn't she been in touch for the past year and where did the weeun come from? Couldn't she have let us know she was expecting? I rolled my eyes at that one. Once a baby is born you just get on with it, no point laying blame and asking how or why.

Our Scarlett wasn't too happy by the looks of her. She said she had been sick with the pregnancy and hadn't been able to travel. She didn't want to tell us she was pregnant in a letter so she thought it was best to wait until she could face us in person and come to visit us to let us see the baby.

That was all well and good but over the next few days she talked about going on the road again. She had the chance of singing back-up for some big band and she couldn't miss the opportunity. Your granddad knew what was coming next; she wanted us to look after you for a couple of weeks, maybe a month or so at the most.

That was all right with me. I didn't want to see Scarlett leave again, thought she might have wised-up and settled down, now she had a baby, but when I realised she wasn't to be persuaded to stay I was more than happy to have you to look after.

Your granddad was a different matter. Oh, we had strong words over it I must say. He thought if we said no, Scarlett would catch herself on and stay put. But I knew Scarlett, and I was too frightened she would just take flight with you and we'd never see her or you again, and that wouldn't be fair on any of us. He said then we would give her an ultimatum, that we would bring you up, keep you here with us and that she could come and go as she pleased but by all intents and purposes you were to be ours. He wanted no rows over how you were to be brought up.

So, we agreed to put it to her and she agreed, not at first but she came around to the idea. Trouble was your granddad was calling her bluff, he thought she would have said no and stayed in Belfast instead. He said all this chasing the spotlight was over, she had a baby now to look after, and it was time she realised she couldn't have both.

The next morning, we woke up to find Scarlett gone and you mewling like a wee cat in the bottom drawer. She left a note; it's in the box for you to read. Just said she had to go back on the road and that she would send money whenever she could.

Ava rummaged through the photographs and newspaper cuttings to find the note again. There it was written in precise, sharp, angular letters on lemony yellow notepaper with a floral border.

Sorry I had to run out like this but I can't stand saying goodbye. Look after Ruby for me. I will send money for her keep as soon as I can.

Your daughter Scarlett x

She sent money home, a brave sum every month, but your granddad wouldn't cash the cheques, said we didn't need her handouts if she couldn't settle herself at home and make do with a terrace house and a good Northern Irish husband she could go to hell or LA, whichever came first. He was a stubborn man your grandfather. Course problem was he'd lost his baby girl. She had grown up and taken flight and he wasn't a bit pleased about it. So, I says nothing, keeps my counsel to myself thinking she'll come home when she's ready.

But then we didn't bargain for what happened next.

She only went and got herself a record deal. Some swanky Yank took her under his wing and said he would take her all the way to the top. And he did, in more than one way. Her head was right turned by him and poor Johnny was long left behind.

Came to see me a few years later as it happens. Nice lad really. Would have been a good husband in spite of all his posturing. Once he grew up and got rid of the long hair and the too-tight blue jeans, he looked like a nice respectable fella. Ended up teaching at some posh grammar school in Bangor. I saw him on the telly one night being interviewed by that fella who does the news on UTV going on about the eleven-plus. I would've recognised his face anywhere. Scarlett might have done all right if she had hung onto Johnny.

Anyway, the Yank, Jackson was his name, got her the record deal and organised a tour. She was to be the new Stevie Nicks, whoever he was. I would have preferred her to stay in Ireland and done the Eurovision like Dana but sure she never listened to me.

The album did well; I have a copy put aside for you, not my type of thing but then I was old before my time, as they say. They did their tour supporting some group named Styx and she did well enough across the Atlantic. Still, I don't think it was all a bed of roses. We didn't hear much from her and the press cuttings soon dried up — you'll find them in a scrapbook I put together over the years for you.

I think after a while she felt she couldn't come back. You were doing well at school and were right settled with me. She could hardly come swanning in and steal you away now, could she? Especially not if the big dream hadn't lasted and I don't think it did, to tell the truth.

Your granddad was a proud and stubborn man. Didn't understand how his wee girl had gone from wearing her hair in ringlets for the Irish dancing to some stuck up little madam who had stars in her eyes when she should have been looking after you. It near enough killed him and just before your fourth birthday, he dropped down dead in the middle of watching of Political Eye.

I contacted Scarlett, she had left a couple of American telephone numbers for emergencies and after a bit of explaining and being passed from one person to another, I eventually got hold of her, and she flew home for the funeral a day later.

She didn't stay long, said she had recording commitments which she was 'contractually obliged to fulfil', was how she put it, and I wasn't going to beg. I had too much to do, what with the funeral only just over, and you to look after. So off she went again and left me to care for you and sort out all the stuff that comes with the death of someone you love.

I was cleaning in the big posh houses up the Malone Road to make ends meet.

A few months later, she came back, wanted to spend some time with you, she said. Your wee face lit up when you saw the stuff she bought you: dresses, wee cowboy boots and a good wool coat, red it was with a velvet collar, toys and such like. Lovely stuff like you wouldn't have seen over here. Next thing I knew, she had gone and bought a house and not just any old house. Dr McCooley's house, the one I used to clean, had come on the market and Scarlett had gone and bought it, just like that. I couldn't believe it. Said she wanted us to live in it and she would come and go when she got the chance.

Not on your life, says I, you have this youngster confused enough as it is, settle yourself and if you want to we can all get along great in that big house. But no, she wouldn't hear of it, said she needed to work for her soul. Did you ever hear the likes of it? I told her the only thing her soul needed was an hour in the confessional and a couple of decades of the rosary.

Thought I'd call her bluff like granddad did and told her she could stay home or take herself off for good. I wasn't best pleased with the way she thought she could just arrive as if she was the answer to all our prayers and up sticks and leave when it suited. Besides, it wasn't good for you. Your wee heart broke every time she left, and I had had enough of drying your tears.

So, she did, just went. Left paperwork stating the house had been signed over to me. Of course, I couldn't bring myself to live in it without Scarlett. What would you and I have done in yon big house? We'd have rattled around like two spools of thread in an empty Quality Street tin. So anyways, the house lay empty. I didn't even set foot in it. Didn't need to see it since I had cleaned it often enough for the McCooleys when they lived there. I wasn't going to start pretending I was lady of the manor or any such thing.

When I had that wee turn last June, I realised I needed to sort out everything so that if the worst should have happened, you would be able to find the paperwork and make sense of it all. I never ever want to be a burden on you so the Sisters of Mercy have been good enough to give me a place. They will offer up the burden of looking after me to the divine grace, so at least for them, I will be a useful burden.

When the time comes, you can decide what to do with the big house. It's rightfully yours. Scarlett wanted you to grow-up in it but I didn't think it was right for a wee girl to have such a big place. We would have only been lonely there and sure we wouldn't have had anything in common with the neighbours. I am sure you'll agree we were both as well off in Moonstone Street as anywhere. That wee house has served its purpose.

Chapter 8

Scarlett examined her face in the glittery, junk-shop bought mirror hanging over her bathroom sink. The lines around her eyes were deepening into grooves and the texture of her skin was becoming a little more, well, *leathery*. God, she hated this ageing process.

She didn't expect to stay twenty-one forever, but neither had she expected to feel the ravages of time quite so painfully. She would have thought that having gone through all she had over the last few years, a couple of wrinkles wouldn't have worried her but vanity was a strange bed partner. Just when you hoped it was asleep or better still dead, it would rear its ugly head and make you feel insecure and vulnerable, dragging you down into the depths of self-loathing.

Scarlett continued massaging the gloopy bee sting serum into her skin. God knows she needed all the help she could get. Part of the problem lay in this place. It was full of glamorous, well-kept and surgically enhanced women. Grooming in LA, unlike her native Belfast, was not the reserve of horses or dogs. To appear without make-up was perfectly acceptable providing your nails were polished, your bikini line waxed within an inch of indecency and your hair was as silky and shiny as a dressage horse's.

Scarlett worked out every day. Runs along the beachfront ensured she was toned and supple. She did yoga twice a week and even taught the odd class to help her friend Stella out when she was out of town.

No one could say Scarlett didn't work at it, but since she had hit forty-eight, she seemed to be losing the battle. She continued to dye her hair but, on her stylist's advice, had moved from inky black to deepest conker in the hope of softening her colouring to help her face look less haggard. She shopped in all the trendy vintage shops and maintained a "with it" attitude. She knew the scene. But really, if she was totally honest, she knew it was time to call it a day.

The entertainment industry required everyone to either be eighteen, look like they could be, or were at least trying hard to stay young. Thank God, she had an alternative outlet for her creativity. These days she was happier creating beautiful pieces of jewellery bespoke for the individual wearer. Her days of gigging had long passed.

The previous week, she had relished the attentions of a thirty-something ride, thinking he was hitting on her, only for him to tell her his mother used to listen to her music in the car going to soccer practice. Oh life, why *so cruel?*

Scarlett picked up the little toolbox, stocked with wire, cutters, pliers and beads, which she used for making jewellery when she wanted to sit outside. For days now, her mind was whirling over thoughts of the past. Things she assumed she had long forgotten, caught her unawares, making her stop whatever it was she was doing, and to think about home. Funny how after all this time she still called it home.

Just a couple of days earlier, she had had an urgent wake up call. Her lawyers had written to her instructing her that the house she had bought for her mother in Belfast had been signed over to Ava. Maggie must have finally died. The realisation that life had moved on at such an accelerated pace during her absence was like an electric jolt of awakening. Somehow, in her screwed-up head, she had thought that life in Belfast would be frozen, waiting for her to return and pick up where she left off. Of course, she wasn't so flaky as to actually believe it be so, but part of her couldn't imagine them moving on without her. God, for all she knew, Ava could have children by now. Scarlett could actually be a grandmother. She shuddered at the thought of it.

When Scarlett received the letter full of legalese, she had cried. Not real sobbing crying, but she had shed a little tear. Maggie had never understood Scarlett. All her life she had battled against her mother and the sense that Maggie was trying to dampen down her enthusiasm for life. But there was no holding Scarlett back. She had fought against her parents' small-minded outlook on life and taken off before either of them could crush the spirit out of her.

God, the nights she'd lain in that shoebox of a house in Moonstone Street, dreaming of a better life. She couldn't bear the feeling of the four walls closing in on her. Even now, thinking of that little house made her feel claustrophobic and breathless.

She had always felt that there was more to life than small-minded bigotry, mass on a Sunday, and settling down to marry some boy you had known for half your life. Scarlett never settled for anyone. Not even Johnny, and with hindsight, she recognised he had been the love of her life. Johnny Kavanagh with his long wavy hair and kind blue eyes which seemed to bore into her very heart. He had treated Scarlett well, even when she had hurt him deeply. He would have been there for her if she had asked.

It was a time of revolution for women everywhere in the world, bar Belfast. She wanted to feel the freedom and the sense of self that she read about. An intense power struggle raged on within her — the need to break out and find something worth living for, taking risks and pulling against the demands of being the dutiful daughter. In the end, there wasn't much of a tug of war, the dutiful daughter had been let go with ease, and they waved off the eager to see the world Scarlett, expecting her to return with her tail between her legs.

Her voice was her ticket out of the backwater she had had the misfortune of being born in. She planned on singing her way to a better life and to a certain extent she did. There had been high points, hearing her song on the radio, doing gigs, touring. She had loved it all. But it had come at a price. A high price.

She knew she had missed out on Ava. She could still close her eyes and conjure up the smell and the feel of that soft, downy head. That crushing ache would never ease, but she felt back then that she had no choice but to leave her behind. The road wasn't practical or safe for a baby. She was working nights, sleeping days, and moving from one town and one relationship to another. Her career was about to soar and looking after a baby wouldn't have worked out at all.

She wanted the best for Ava too. Leaving her with Maggie wouldn't have been the worst scenario. She had made sure they were financially looked after. The McCooley house had cost a fortune but she had been proud to give it to her mother. At least Ava didn't have to grow up in the suffocating house on Moonstone Street.

Scarlett had often longed to go back, just to check in and see the little girl but she knew better than to cross Maggie. They had agreed. If Maggie was going to bring her up she didn't want Scarlett's interference. Besides, it was too painful to flit in and out. She had been choked up with emotion leaving after her dad's funeral. The flight back to the States had been agony. She had sobbed uncontrollably as if she had lost them all, not just her father.

But now, Maggie had gone. Scarlett thought that Ava would have contacted her. Surely, she deserved to go to the funeral and say her goodbyes?

But she didn't blame Ava. Of course, she was probably resentful. She most likely felt rejected but Scarlett could explain, tell her how it had been back then, how she had so much to do with her life and that she wasn't ready to be a mother. Maybe Ava would find it in her heart to understand and let her try again.

Scarlett appreciated the peace and quiet she had found in making jewellery. Ruby Red Heart was the name of her little company. Funny, really, to even think of it as a business but her friend Adam had helped her set up a website, and she was surprised at the orders coming in from as far away as Rome.

Her USP, or *unique selling point* — she had laughed at the business speak — was that the jewellery was made with a specific need in mind. If someone had trouble dealing with emotional imbalance, problems of self-esteem, or lacking in confidence, then Scarlett would select moss agate crystals and make a piece of jewellery with the stones entwined. She had several emails and letters thanking her not just for the beauty of her pieces but for her help in addressing issues troubling the wearer.

Scarlett sat with her back to the old white-washed fence and looked out to the sea, while she braided the gold wire, and threaded on tiny topaz and crystal stones. She was working on a specially requested bracelet for a lonely woman who had allowed her alcohol dependency to push away all her friends. The woman was seeking companionship. She needed support and warmth. Topaz, the November birthstone, brought friendship and trust, while the amethyst crystals were considered to be a strong antidote to alcohol.

Scarlett thought of the origins of the stones she was working with, how the Greek word amethystos means "not drunken", and that amethysts were inlaid in wine goblets used by clergy in ancient times. It was also believed that the amethysts could increase intelligence and dispel evil or negative thoughts. Perfect for a woman trying to recover from alcoholism. As a healing crystal, amethyst could be uplifting and help strengthen both the endocrine and immune systems while aiding the pituitary gland and being a powerful blood cleaner and energiser. Scarlett would take time to explain all of this to the wearer when she came to collect her piece of jewellery.

The stones shimmered and twinkled in the sunlight, throwing prisms of light onto her bare golden-tanned arms. Scarlett breathed in deeply, holding on for a second longer than necessary as if to savour the very air surrounding her. Everything she did these days seemed imbued with longing. She missed this place before she was even gone from it. The truth was that she knew to go back was to give all this up. She could no longer flit. It would be time to stay and face the music, even if she didn't pick the soundtrack herself. She would have to dance to someone else's rhythm. But maybe that wasn't such a bad thing. Maybe she would find comfort in watching her daughter dance through life instead.

Chapter 9

Ava tapped the cost of the wreath into the till. Fifty-two pounds for a guitar made out of flowers, to be laid on a music loving, teenager's grave.

His mother had seemed embarrassed when she had come in the day before requesting the arrangement. He loved his guitar, she said, her eyes moist and bloodshot with tears already spent. She agreed to collect it the following day. It would have been his sixteenth birthday. She wanted to buy him a present and this was all she could think of.

Ava had chosen the textured foliage with purple larkspur and irises with deep pink chrysanthemums to create it. She had listened to the mother recount how her son had loved playing his guitar and never paid much attention to her no matter how often she nagged him to put it down and go and do some studying. Now she wished she had listened to his strumming more intently for the house was so quiet without him.

Ava handed the woman her change and let her put it into her purse before placing the flower arrangement into her arms which she handled as carefully as she would have a newborn baby.

Ava hadn't asked how he died. It was bad enough to know that such grief existed without sharing in the details. She sighed as she cleared up for the day then decided to send Joseph a text.

Ava: *Hey, how are you? Long-time no hear.*
Joseph: *Cool. Working hard.*
Ava: *How's my damp squib emoji coming on?*
Joseph: *In production as I text. Should be coming to an iPhone near you, any day now.*

Ava: *So, still living like an American?*

Joseph: *What you mean working twelve-hour days, eating clean and going for a run at lunchtime? Yeah. Still living like an American.*

Ava: *I won't recognise you when you come home next. You'll be all fresh faced, glossed and groomed.*

Joseph: *Nah, I still look like an Irish reject. I swear to God my accent gets stronger the longer I'm here. I think I do it unconsciously to wind the Yanks up, you know?*

Ava: *Does it work?*

Joseph: *Nope. I think they like it. How's Maggie doing? My mum said she's not been too well.*

Ava: *Not bad. The stroke has affected her down one side but she still manages to give out orders and boss me around.*

Joseph: *God, do you remember the time she nearly caught us drinking cider? I thought she'd skin me alive. Her precious Ava could do no wrong. I would've definitely got the blame.*

Ava: *Thank God she bought your story that it was a new type of soda stream. What was it you called it?*

Joseph: *Apple Jumping Jack. I should have gone into marketing.*

Ava: *Got to run – a customer's popped in. Talk soon.*

Hazel would be back shortly to add up the day's takings and lock up for the night. Since she had come back from Sorrento, she had been acting kind of strange.

At times, Ava wondered could Hazel have found out about her and Ben, but she felt sure Hazel would have had it out with her rather than sulk over the matter. Besides, Ben had sworn that she wouldn't hear anything from him or Daniel, who's secrecy had been secured with the threat of having his stash of cannabis, which was hidden under his floorboards, uncovered.

The over doorbell jangled as Hazel came dashing in, her hair messed up and her face without a scrap of make-up. Ava could never remember seeing Hazel without her usual covering of foundation, bronzed cheekbones, peachy-coloured lips and lashes of mascara. Something was definitely not right. She bustled about the shop as if she had a purpose but seemed to be doing nothing more than tweaking displays and moving the squat jars of delicious-smelling candles around without even taking her coat off.

'Right you, sit down and tell me what's up,' Ava instructed, locking the door and turning the sign to closed.

Hazel didn't even try to deny there was a problem. Her shoulders quivered and she suddenly filled up, her eyes looking tired and piggy small without their usual cosmetic enhancement.

'Oh, Ava. I don't know what to do.' She took off her expensive camel-coloured mohair coat and draped it over the shop counter, not caring that it could be stained by the sodden block of oasis or the ends of greenery still waiting to be cleared away.

She sat down on the seat behind the till and began crying nosily. She honked her nose into a tissue as Ava put her arm around her.

'What's wrong? Please tell me. If it's Ben then I'll understand if you want me to go, but just hear me out first.'

'Ben? What's it to do with our Ben? No. Robert. My Robert has only gone and… and…' She broke off into another sobbing fit.

'What's Robert done? Sure, haven't the two of you just come back from a second honeymoon in Sorrento? You were full of the joys of spring.'

'You see that's what he would like me to think too. Oh, typical tactic, spoil the little wife with presents and compliments to stop her being suspicious, but *I'm* onto him,' she said, her eyes gleaming with sadness and hurt and a definite edge of bitterness.

'And what's more he waited 'til I had hit my *time* before he went and did it. He knew I was worried and feeling sensitive about it, when all along he had been thinking that it was time for him to find a replacement,' she howled.

'Hazel you aren't making any sense. What time have you hit and what has your Robert done?' Ava asked, wondering where on earth this was going.

Hazel blew her nose again and tried to steady herself. 'I've reached that time in a woman's life when *it* is starting to pass.'

Ava looked at Hazel's blotchy red face. 'I might sound a bit dense here, but what the hell are you on about?'

'I'm starting to dry up. I'm *past it*. I'm going through the *menopause*,' she whispered as if in mortal fear of causing offence to delicate ears.

'But that isn't the end of the world. Sure, can't you get HRT off the doctor?' asked Ava, trying to sound sympathetic.

'That would be all well and good except my husband knows that I'm reaching the Helen Mirren stage of life, and instead of being supportive, he's looked elsewhere to trade up. He's probably with some Jennifer Lawrence or Margot Robbie lookalike right now,' she wailed.

Ava handed her another tissue and let her continue.

'You see, I was the fool who confided in him. Told him I was losing my monthlies, I had put on a bit of weight and getting the hot flushes, so I was. I could see myself going like my poor mother who lost her figure overnight when she went through the change. Says he, I'll take you on a wee holiday to lift your spirits like and you'll feel like a new woman, when all along it was him that felt like a new bloody woman, and then he only went and took one back to my marital bed!'

'No! Robert would never do that. He loves the bones of you, Hazel,' said Ava, stunned to think that the rotund Robert could pull anything let alone would be stupid enough to try to cheat on the glamorous and attractive Hazel.

'You would think that but I have *proof*!' She looked up with a crazed look in her wet eyes. 'I found a cheap-looking necklace in my bed. Explain that to me, ha! Takes me on a romantic holiday to ease his conscience and while I'm working away all the hours of the day here, he has had some wee bit of fluff in *my bed*.' She wailed like a banshee on the brink of midnight, throwing her manicured hands up into the air in anger.

'To think I put clean sheets on the bed for some wee harlot to have her way with my husband on my lovely John Rocha cotton percale sheets.'

Ava blinked rapidly in horror as she suddenly remembered how Niamh had complained that Ava had lost her necklace, lent as part of the operation recovery makeover. She shuddered as she realised it must have been Hazel's bed she had slept in with Ben.

Shit, shit, shit. She would have to come clean to save her friend from thinking her husband had done the dirty on her, but her heart lurched at the thought of confessing to her fling with Ben.

'Now, Hazel, be realistic. There is bound to be a reasonable explanation. You shouldn't be jumping to conclusions. Marriage is about trust, after all. Don't tell me you are going to doubt the man who worships the ground you walk on,' said Ava, trying to keep her voice calm while wracking her brain to come up with an explanation that wouldn't involve her having wild, messy, dirty sex with Hazel's son, in Hazel's two hundred thread count Egyptian sheets.

'Whatever you do, don't say anything to Robert yet. Let's think about this and get all the angles covered before you accuse him of something he hasn't done,' reasoned Ava, 'and book yourself an appointment with the doctor. No point going through the change without finding out if you can take something to help with all the symptoms. I promise you that there is no way that Robert has slept with someone else. Trust me.'

Ava was racked with guilt. How could she have let this happen? It was practically divine retribution — she had to watch her dear friend break her heart, devastated to think that her husband was having an affair.

Ava was the guilty party. She didn't know which would be worse for Hazel, thinking that Robert had strayed or that her precious son had slept with the hired help. Oh God, why did she let this stupid mess happen, and how was she going to resolve it?

Chapter 10

Now that Ava knew Scarlett had bought Mount Pleasant Square for her and her gran, she was more determined than ever to live in it. She spent every spare minute there, sanding down wood panelling and scrubbing windows. It consumed her. Niamh and Cal knew she had inherited an old house, but they didn't know anything beyond that. Ava wasn't ready to tell them that Scarlett had been the mysterious benefactor.

Ava had followed Amanda's advice to take out a smallish mortgage on the property to cover the necessary work to make it habitable. The mortgage had come through, and she had instructed the builder, Phil, to start with the renovations. So far, he had gutted out the kitchen and the main bathroom, replaced some missing roof tiles and plastered some of the worst of the walls. Already it felt different, more like a home than the run-down house it was. Money was tight but she was determined to make it habitable.

Meeting Ben at Mount Pleasant Square had been the safest way of ensuring that no one saw them together. Belfast was a small town in many respects, and Ava didn't want Hazel to hear about their liaison from anyone but herself. But before she went ahead and told all, she needed to clarify the story with Ben or try to at least find a good cover.

There had to be a way of explaining how the necklace had ended up in Hazel's bed without giving away the *whole* truth. If they could make her see reason, that Robert had not cheated on her, then it would be worth the risk of their exposure but having witnessed the wrath of Hazel's heartbreak, Ava did not wish to put herself in the firing line unless she absolutely had to. Besides, nothing had happened with Ben since then. She had resisted his sexy texts and late-night phone calls and had chalked it up to experience — of which she had had little to make comparisons. How Niamh managed to weave her tangled web of relationships was so far outside of Ava's reality that she cringed at the thought of the lies, the messy cover-ups and the guilt involved. She couldn't lead Niamh's life no matter how adventurous she made it seem.

Niamh and Cal had thought it was the perfect remedy to getting over Finlay. Their only lament had been that they were sworn to secrecy and couldn't spread the gossip about town for it to run Finlay's way, and make him jealous to know Ava had pulled a gorgeous fella, almost ten years her junior.

When Ava had berated Niamh yet again for allowing her to get in such a state that she had gone home with Ben, Niamh had merely chuckled and said, 'Ava, you were all over him like a bad case of herpes.'

Ava had put her hands to her face in shame, saying, 'I'm a bad person. I've slept with my employer and friend's son and to make it worse he's near enough ten years younger than me.'

'Honey pie, when you get to our age — and I know we don't feel old at almost thirty — there is a national shortage of available livestock. You see the best ones are usually in the first flush of marital bliss, still shagging on a weekly basis, and thinking this is forever.' She paused to take a dramatic drag on her cigarette like Joan Collins in her heyday. 'So that leaves the over forties to which I admit, I'm partial to myself. True they have been round the block and usually have one failed marriage behind them, or are at least in the throes of the martial demise, but still they are out there for the taking. But you, darling girl, struck love gold. You managed to get yourself a bit of live bait, still fresh and unburdened by a mortgage and two kiddies. So, don't come moaning to your Auntie Niamh.' She flicked her ash into the saucer which Ava had left out for that very purpose.

Ava huffily lifted the saucer to empty it of its smouldering contents.

She would just have to accept that Niamh wasn't going to be sympathetic to her predicament.

Ava stopped off to buy candles on the way to number ninety-seven. The electrician, Ted, was in the middle of the rewiring job and the electric was still off. She was filled with anxiety every time she checked her bank account. The normally thrifty Ava was haemorrhaging money like she had never done before. It wasn't that she was usually tight with her finances, it was just that previously she had never found anything too big to buy. When she lived at home with Maggie, the pair of them required very little to live on. Ava wasn't one for shopping and buying stuff she didn't need despite the fact that Niamh implored her to spend like money was going out of fashion. She could never get her head around how Niamh required a new outfit every other week, accessories and all. No wonder her apartment was coming down with handbags, jewellery and clothes, and most of them only ever saw the light of day once before being cast off as last season. Still, Ava couldn't complain as many of the less outrageous items found a home in her own wardrobe.

She had yet to buy any furniture seeing as every penny she had ever saved was going into the big remodelling and fixing up jobs, so she spread an old tartan blanket on the woodblock floor in the living room and placed the candles in the fireplace to give them a bit of light to chat by. The candles burning in the grate cast a cosy golden glow around the room, hiding the fact that it was actually very dusty and shabby. No matter how many times she swept a yard brush over the floor, dust would settle again as soon as the workmen left for the day. The wallpaper had been ripped off in patches, exposing the powdery plaster underneath. The bare pinky-coloured walls made Ava think of a newborn baby waiting to be clothed. She hadn't even considered paint colours yet but she was sure Niamh and Cal would have plenty of ideas, desperate as they were to sway her away from neutral greys and soft natural tones.

She had phoned Ben earlier in the day telling him she needed to see him. It wasn't until later that evening that she realised he could have assumed that she wanted to see him for all the wrong reasons, but she would risk hurting his pride to discuss how they could best present the situation to Hazel.

Since Hazel's hysterics over her fears of Robert having an affair, Ava had been eaten up with guilt. It was bad enough to have shagged Ben, but for poor Hazel to believe her beloved Robert had strayed and to do so in her own bed was just beyond cruel. Why Ava hadn't 'fessed up immediately she didn't know. It would have been the right thing to do, but these days Ava surprised herself by not always instinctively doing the right thing. She was a mixed-up mess of late.

At least the whole Ben encounter had helped distract her from Finlay. Niamh had heard from someone in the Gaelic club that he was seeing a girl called Rose. She was a secretary in the same building he worked in and apparently modelled part-time. Ava had picked over the scant details torturing herself, imagining them together in a sexy clinch. Most likely she was the same blonde girl Ava had seen getting out of Finlay's car that night.

One night, in a moment of weakness, Ava had called him. Just to chat she had said, see how he was doing. He had asked about Maggie, talked about work. He had been friendly enough but hadn't mentioned any Rose. They had ended the call, promising to get together for drink sometime but no firm arrangement had been made. It was like talking to an old friend, not someone she had been intimate with and had considered spending the rest of her life with.

Ava looked around the room. She had brushed the worse of the dust and the cobwebs away. It was funny to think number ninety-seven was still a secret of sorts. She had told Maggie that she had inherited a wonderful, old falling down house and was thinking of moving out of Moonstone Street, but she wasn't sure how much Maggie understood these days. She had sat smiling, her face sunken and contorted and had reached over to pat Ava's knee. Ava had chosen to take the gesture as a sign of approval.

Ben would actually be one of her first visitors. She sat down on the blanket and hugged her knees into her chest, trying to imagine how one day she would be sitting on a real sofa in front of a proper fire on this very spot.

'Did you win the lotto or something?' Ben asked as Ava led him into her entrance hall a short while later.

'It's a long story. Come on in. I haven't actually moved in yet as I haven't any furniture and there is a lot of work needs doing, but I thought it was better to meet you here just in case your mum would turn up at my house or someone would see you,' Ava explained in a stammering rush. The sight of his broad shoulders was enough to make her smile with delight. She tried to keep herself in check and to not let her imagination stray.

'Here, I bought you some wine. I figured the last thing you would want would be a bunch of flowers seeing as you work with them all day.' He handed Ava a bottle of Chablis. Probably nicked out of his father's wine collection, thought Ava, accepting the bottle graciously.

'Thanks, but I'm not sure if I have anything we could drink out of, and I probably don't even have a bottle opener,' said Ava, going into the kitchen to see if she could find anything. She unearthed two mugs probably left by the electricians while Ben tried to uncork the bottle with an attachment on his key ring.

They made their way back into the living room where the flickering candles and the blanket spread out on the floor suddenly looked like a scene of hot seduction.

'To us,' said Ben, grinning as he raised his mug in a toast and settled himself down on the blanket.

'Oh no, you don't. I've told you there *is* no us,' said Ava. 'This is strictly business, mister. We're in trouble and I've asked you here to see if we can conjure up a plausible story between us.'

'What's going on?' Ben asked.

'It's your mum. She found my necklace in her bed and now she thinks your dad is having an affair. You need to convince her that it belongs to one of your girlfriends and not to some wee bit of strumpet your dad has picked up.'

Ben snorted. 'But it does belong to one of my girlfriends — you.' He took Ava's face in his hands and moved in to kiss her.

'Ben, I'm not your girlfriend. We had one drunken night which is best forgotten.' She pushed his hands away and saw a flicker of hurt pass over his oh-too-good-looking face.

'Hey come on, you know I'd be up for it if I weren't friends with your mum, but really put yourself in my position. How can I work with her knowing? She would be furious if she had any idea I'd had sex with her precious son,' said Ava trying to let him down gently and convince herself all over again that this was a bad idea. He was so attractive in the soft candlelight. His jawline had a light rough-to-the-touch shadow and his hair a shade of dirty fair, verging on butterscotch, was cut short.

He lay back on the blanket, cocky and sure of himself again.

'Don't sweat it. I'll say I brought home Mickey. She'll be that pissed at the thought of me going out with Mickey again, that she'll forgive me for using her bed.'

Relief washed over Ava. Ben's ex, the one with the ridiculous name. Yes, that would work. Hazel would be angry at Ben but she would be so relieved that Robert hadn't been unfaithful that she wouldn't be too cross. It was a perfect cover story. Somehow in her elation that it would all work out, Ava found herself leaning over to Ben and placing her lips on his.

Chapter 11

It had been a couple of weeks since Ava had caught up with Niamh and she needed her company. It wasn't that she didn't enjoy seeing Ben, of course she did, but when they got together it inevitably ended up being all about tearing each other's clothes off and being playful. Ava needed a bit of conversation. Number ninety-seven was a mess of building work and Maggie was a bit low, spending most of her days and nights sleeping or staring mournfully out of the window at the lawn. Ava needed to think of something other than electrics, plumbing, incontinence pads and ways to cheer Maggie up.

Niamh was always the perfect antidote for worrying about yourself, she had enough drama for both of them.

'So, tell me all about Ben,' Niamh said helping herself to a fish cake and dipping it into the sweet chilli sauce. She was wearing her canary yellow silk kimono which she had bought when she was on location in Tokyo, the one and only time she had film work beyond Ireland.

'There's really nothing new to report. He's lovely but it's not going anywhere, and I know at some stage I'll have to gently say goodbye but for now it's fun, as long as Hazel doesn't find out that is. I'd die of shame if she knew,' Ava said, her cheeks colouring at the very thought of Hazel knowing what she'd got up to with her son the night before.

'Hey, don't sweat it. She'd probably be a lot cooler about it than you imagine,' Niamh said dishing out more noodles onto her plate.

'I'm not so sure. Ben is her blue-eyed boy. I can't imagine she would approve of me corrupting him,' said Ava finishing off her drink.

Niamh snorted with laughter. 'Sorry but I just can't imagine you corrupting anyone, Miss Goody Two Shoes, who's never done a bad, or dirty thing in her life.'

'Oh, don't be so sure,' Ava said. 'Maybe I have a secret kinky sex life you know nothing about. I could be into bondage and all sorts, for all you know.'

'Ava Connors, I can't believe you would even joke about having a life I know nothing about,' Niamh said, filling up Ava's glass with more wine.

'So, how's the house coming on?'

'Slowly. Urgh, don't talk to me about builders. What looks like a straightforward one-man job becomes a project needing twenty experts. Still, I know it isn't really their fault. It's just sometimes I wonder what the hell I'm doing. I took a mortgage out against it to cover the cost of the work, but it's like a money pit.'

'Oh, come on it will be fabulous when it's finished. You are one lucky girl,' Niamh said. Ava knew Niamh couldn't wait for the house to be ready for her and Cal to launch their style makeover on it. They were surreptitiously working hard to dissuade Ava away from chintzy Laura Ashley prints and inferior William Morris wallpaper copies.

Ava sipped her wine. 'That's *if* it ever gets finished, I'm running out of money fast. Who would have thought damp proofing could cost so much, and don't get me started on the electrics.'

'Still, what an inheritance. I wish someone would leave me a big house in Malone, whether it was in disrepair or not.'

'Let's not talk about the house. The speed at which it is drinking up money is depressing me. Cheer me up with some scandal,' Ava said as The Killers playlist switched to The Script.

Niamh grinned. 'Now you mention it, I may have a piece of juicy gossip.'

'Do tell. I'm all ears as long as it doesn't involve Finlay.'

'Don't worry it's nothing to do with Finlay Kane. Do you remember Colm Ferguson from school?' She leaned in towards Ava, Niamh's cropped pinky-blonde hair catching the light.

'Who? Colm with the red hair who defied nature by still managing to be completely gorgeous? Wasn't he a couple of years above us? Just about everyone fancied him.'

Niamh nodded. 'Yep the same one. I... sort of ran into him. A few times.'

'When you say ran into him, do you mean ran him over before you jumped his sexy bones?'

'Oh, you know me so well.'

'Hang on a minute, didn't he marry Carey Cunningham?' Ava asked. Carey Cunningham had a reputation, probably unfounded, for her blowjobs when the rest of the girls in lower sixth where only starting to work out that there was no blow in blow job. Carey had the most gorgeous pillowy lips which had been deemed the blow-up doll pout, probably explaining how her reputation came to be.

'Mmm. I heard something about it, but it can't be a good marriage if he's out playing with other women, namely *moi*.'

'*Oh Niamh*, please don't tell me you are shagging a married man again,' Ava admonished. Sometimes she despaired of Niamh's inability to play fairly. In Ava's mind, married men were out of bounds. She wouldn't even contemplate the thought of an affair, even if he were gorgeous looking.

'Don't go all judgemental on me. I really like him, Ava. What if this time it's different?' Niamh said, her voice suddenly low and quiet.

'How can it possibly be different? He's taken. *End of*. People will be hurt. You can't just mess up someone's life because you fancy their husband. Besides, if it feels so different that only means you are bound to wind up getting hurt as well.'

Niamh cast her eyes down and sulked. She was chewing on her thumbnail looking like the injured party.

'At least tell me he has no kids,' Ava said wearily.

Niamh mumbled something.

'What did you say?'

'Just the one.'

'Oh, Niamh no, please, you have to end this before it goes too far.'

'I don't think I can.' She turned to Ava with her heavily made-up eyes brimming with unshed tears. 'He phoned me earlier to say he thinks Carey might have found out about us.'

Ava couldn't explain Niamh's fixation on wanting what she couldn't have. She had jumped from one bad relationship to the other over the years and invariably ended up crying to Ava.

'Look, maybe she hasn't really found out and you can end it before anyone needs to get hurt. Please, Niamh, think about his child. There is someone out there for you who doesn't have a wife and a family, hold out and stop finding yourself married men.' Ava sighed. It was no use lecturing Niamh, she was a big girl and was capable of making her own choices. Besides, Ava didn't feel so holier than thou when she thought of her relationship with Ben. He may not be married but she still felt that she was betraying Hazel by sleeping with her son.

Then there was the whole issue of their age difference. It wasn't as if she could even claim he was mature for his years. He liked video games, was addicted to his iPhone, loved to go clubbing, did the whole festival scene in the summer, and thought nothing of drinking Red Bull for breakfast to wash down a jammy doughnut.

They were miles apart in so many ways yet she had to admit she liked him. More than liked him.

For once, she didn't feel morally superior to Niamh's antics. Maybe they were both going to hell for their betrayals.

Chapter 12

'Hey, why so sad?' asked Sister Lucy as Ava sat in the armchair watching Maggie sleep. 'She's only asleep you know. There's been no change. The rest will do her good.'

'Oh, I know. She's strong and determined. I just hate seeing her like this.' Ava brushed a tear from her cheek and took a deep breath to prevent her from sobbing all over poor Sister Lucy.

The truth was, seeing Maggie like this reminded Ava that her gran was close to death and that thought was terrifying. It was as if death was sucking the very breath from her lungs, as Ava looked on, watching her slowly ebb away. She seemed as vulnerable and helpless as a newborn baby.

'It's just that she has always been there for me. She brought me up and I can't imagine a time when she won't be here. I know I haven't had her for a while now, not really, but at least I can come here and chat to her, brush her hair or change the flowers and tidy her room.'

'Death is the one inevitability of life, Ava. We all return to our Lord. But I know it won't be easy for you. What about your mother, do you have any contact with her?' Sister Lucy sat on the chair beside Ava, her long legs looking almost comically elegant.

'No, but that's something I'm hoping to rectify. I've asked my solicitor to try track her down.'

'Maybe you'll feel better to have her support. It would be good for Maggie to pass on knowing you have your mother in your life again.'

'Oh, it's difficult to know with Gran. I mean she never told me much about my mother. She buried all her worries and thoughts about her, and never shared any of it with me.'

'But don't you see? That was her way of protecting you from feeling any of the hurt or pain she may have felt herself. I'm not saying it was the right thing to do, just that sometimes we do the wrong thing for all the right reasons.'

They sat in companionable silence for a few moments while Ava stroked Maggie's hand. Her skin was tissue-paper thin, exposing the intricate network of violet blue veins, the joints twisted and gnarled by arthritis. Ava thought about the countless times she had held that hand crossing a road. How the same hands could deftly button up her school shirt in a few seconds and stroke her hair as a way of comforting her in the dead of the night when she had dreamt of something scary. How it could give her a whack across the back of her legs for doing something dangerous, and still tenderly bathe her in warm soapy water making sure to never let the suds touch Ava's eyes.

'Sister Lucy, can I ask you a personal question?'

'In for a penny in for a pound, go on then, ask away.'

'Do you ever regret always having to be so good and holy? That sounds awful, I mean having made the choice of giving your life to God, do you ever wonder *what if*?'

'Oh child, no, not at all. My life was mapped out for me. I could no more become an astronaut than turn away from my calling. But if you're asking me about being good, I'll say this: good girls go to heaven, but bad girls, they go *everywhere*.' She gave a little giggle and leapt up to leave the room, leaving Ava with a smile on her face.

Ava: *It arrived! My lil' squid baby.*
Joseph: *Ha ha. I thought you'd appreciate it. Saw it in a little shop on Lower Pacific Heights. It was full of strange stuffed toys. Couldn't believe they actually had a squid. You'd love it in J-Town. It's full of all sorts of weird knick-knacks and collectables.*
Ava: *What's J-Town?*
Joseph: *A whole Japanese enclave. Great food and shops. I'll take you there if I can ever persuade you to come visit me.*

Ava: *Yeah, some day. You know I can't leave Maggie at the minute. She's not been great.*

Joseph: *I know. No pressure, but the offer stands any time. I'll even book you a ticket.*

Ava: *Don't tempt me. In the meantime, I'll have to make do with my stuffed lil squid friend to keep me company.*

Joseph: *Still no Finlay?*

Ava: *Nope. I think it's time I moved on, don't you?*

Joseph: *Yep. Someone out there will appreciate you.*

Ava: *Here's hoping. What about you? Anyone special?*

Nah. American girls are too high maintenance. They're also a bit scary.

Ava: *Can't be any worse than Niamh.*

Ha ha, she'd go down well here actually.

Ava: *Jaysus, can you imagine?*

Joseph: *Sorry. Have to run. I'm on my lunch break which means I'm expected to mingle with my fellow geeks and be productive while I eat my wild rice and yellow fin tuna salad.*

Ava: *Bet you'd love a good old Belfast bap with Tayto cheese and onion crisps and a piece of ham.*

Joseph: *Sounds divine. Talk soon.*

Ava: *Bye!*

Chapter 13

'Wow look at you!' Cal exclaimed opening the door to Niamh's apartment to let Ava in. She was wearing a new pair of skinny dark denim jeans with a tight royal blue T-shirt she had bought from a snazzy little boutique in town with a little black fitted waistcoat over the top. Her legs looked magically slender and longer thanks to the platform boots she had been unable to resist. But even more striking than the clothes was her new hairstyle. She had finally got around to having her hair coloured, a deep cherry red which suited her pale skin tone and made her violet blue eyes vibrant and sparkly.

'Oh. My. God. You have finally got with the programme,' screeched Niamh when she saw the new-look Ava.

'Turn around, let me see.'

Ava dutifully gave a twirl, relishing her friend's approval. She had even invested in some Stila lip gloss, a Bobbi Brown bronzing cheeks and eyes compact, and some tinted moisturiser.

'I've been telling you for years to dye your hair. It looks fantastic. Finlay Kane will be gutted he ever let you go,' Niamh said.

'This is not for Finlay's benefit. It was just time for a change.' Ava had decided that night she would tell Niamh and Cal the whole backstory about ninety-seven Mount Pleasant Square Square, the letter from Maggie, and the unsettling feeling she'd had ever since discovering that Scarlett had intended for her to be named Ruby instead of the boring Ava.

Later, they caught up while Cal and Niamh practiced their arts of deception on Ava.

'So, let me get this right. You told Ben it was a no-go and then jumped him right there and then on the floor of the old derelict house you've just inherited?' Cal asked, his eyes wide.

'More or less. I hadn't planned it. It was just one of those mad moments,' replied Ava, lying on the sofa while Niamh and Cal worked on her face. She was being their practice dummy to help them prep for a gory road accident commercial.

'But, Ava, for as long as I've known you, you don't tend to have moments of madness,' reasoned Niamh, applying a thick layer of sticky glue to Ava's cheek to hold the latex in place.

'And your mother named you Ruby, but Maggie thought it would be too much like tempting fate to give you a name as glamorous as your mother's?' asked Cal.

'Yeah, but you know, the strangest thing is that since I read the letter and began thinking about my mother, I've been feeling… well, *different*. Sort of more like a Ruby and less like an Ava, if that makes any sense.'

'Stay still,' Niamh said, applying blood red paint to the latex wound on Ava's face.

'Are we going to have to start calling you Ruby then?' asked Cal, handing Niamh a thin rabbit-hair make-up brush so soft Ava could barely feel the strokes on her skin.

'God, no. I *am* Ava. It's just, I can't explain it. It is as if there were two possible outcomes for me — one as Ava and one as Ruby.'

'And Ruby is the one who has wild rampant sex with her boss's son,' said Niamh. 'Jaysus and you think my life's complicated!'

'I just know that before the letter, I would have never allowed myself to even consider being with Ben once in a drunken stupor let alone to find myself in that position again.'

'What position was that then, cradle snatcher?' joked Cal. 'On top, doggy style, over and under?'

'Don't! You are making me blush and it'll clash with my new hair colour.' Ava laughed. She felt light-hearted and playful, not her usual contained, calm self. It wasn't that she usually didn't do upbeat and fun, it was more that she was one of life's flat-liners — those who neither experienced highs or lows but travelled through life feeling content and satisfied. Though lately she had to admit the fluttering of euphoria that she kept feeling were like little nuggets of pure rainbow sunshine. She didn't want to be all Pollyanna about it, but even though she was worried about Maggie and the mounting bills for Mount Pleasant Square, life was full of unexpected surprises. Granted not all of them were nice, but still there was something to be said for needing digestive biscuits to appreciate chocolate ones. Ava had eaten enough digestives to do her a lifetime, it was time for her to dunk a big fat chocolaty biscuit into the mug of life.

'So, what made you decide not to sell the house and pocket the money?' asked Niamh, admiring the three-inch gash she had created across Ava's face. 'Here, Cal, photograph this for reference.'

'I could have sold it, continued living in Moonstone Street, and even brought my gran out of the convent and employed a series of full time nurses, but you know what? I don't think that Maggie would have been too happy with me if I'd done that. I know the nuns are looking after her well, and I've no guarantee that I'd find the right carers for her no matter how much I could pay them.'

She sat up and looked at her refection in the mirror. Her face was transformed to resemble something out of a horrific crash. 'Sister Lucy told me at the beginning, when Gran went into the home, that I had to respect her wishes for where she wanted to spend her remaining days. She didn't want me to have to wipe her bum and clean the gunk out of her eyes every morning. She worked too hard all her life to feel that she was holding me back. So, I've sort of accepted it and you know what? For the first time ever, I feel, I dunno, reckless! Does that make any sense?'

'Sister, you go for it,' said Cal clicking the digital camera as he photographed the finished job.

'Besides I was meant to have number ninety-seven. Scarlett had intended for me and Maggie to live there,' Ava said, smiling widely for the camera despite the fact that her face looked like someone had slashed it with a serrated knife.

'So how did it end up with the whole Colm and Carey thing?' Ava asked.

Niamh made a face. 'Must we talk about my disastrous love life?' She slicked on a fresh coat of lip gloss.

'Your disastrous love life keeps me entertained, so humour me and fill me in. I assume you have seen the error of your ways and ended it before anything happened?'

Ava had heard many tales of Niamh's relationships, many which involved compromising positions and having sex in inappropriate places with equally inappropriate, unavailable men. It was a shame Colm Ferguson was married because he was the first man Ava could remember in a long time that Niamh had fancied below the age of forty. Still, he was married and thus should have been out of bounds, and Niamh should have known better than to allow herself to become involved with him.

'He showed up the next day and lit on me like I had ruined his life or something. Told me I wasn't worth losing his family over. You'd have thought I had drugged him and dragged him back to my apartment all three times I shagged the good-for-nothing bastard,' Niamh said, throwing back the last of her drink.

'So how do you feel now?'

'Same as always: like shit,' she replied looking despondent. 'Why do I have to fall for the wrong fellas? It's as if I have a self-destruct button lodged in my heart. I really liked Colm too. I think we could have worked well together.'

'Oh, Niamh, there's someone out there for you who isn't married and doesn't have children. You just have to stop *letting* yourself get hurt like this. You shouldn't allow yourself to be attracted to the wrong type.'

'Ha, you're a fine one to talk. Your love life isn't exactly going well,' Niamh said, studying Ava's make-up wounds.

Chapter 14

'Shut the shop,' ordered Hazel as she rushed in looking like she had just had an encounter with the three witches from Macbeth. Ava could see she had parked her silver Mercedes coupé on the pavement outside, despite the fact that it was on a double yellow line.

'It's the middle of the day. We can't just shut up shop and lose customers,' said Ava, panicked as to why Hazel was looking so demented. She still broke out in a cold sweat every time Hazel looked at her the wrong way for fear she knew about her and Ben.

Hazel went out to the back kitchen where they had a wider counter space to make up larger flower arrangements and flopped down on the old threadbare armchair in the corner. 'I can't believe it,' she said staring straight ahead, wide eyed.

'Hazel come on, you're worrying me. What's going on? It can't be Robert, sure, didn't you tell me Ben had brought Mickey back for one last night of passion while you were in Sorrento, so you know where that necklace came from and that your Robert wasn't playing away.'

'It isn't Robert. I've just been to the doctors to see if I was really going through the change,' she said, her voice unnaturally high and quivering.

'Oh God, Hazel, what is it? You're scaring the life out of me here. Are you all right?'

Hazel looked straight at ahead, her eyes glazed over. 'I'm pregnant,' she answered, suddenly quiet and childlike.

Half an hour later, the shop was locked up with a hastily scrawled sign saying, '*Closed due to family emergency*' stuck on the door and they were settled into their favourite booth in Madison's. Usually lunches out in Madison's were reserved for real treats when they had worked flat out over Valentine's Day or were celebrating a special birthday, but even then, they left the shop in the capable hands of Erin who did the odd bit of part-time work for them when they needed extra help.

Ava was sipping brandy and lemonade while Hazel had a large glass of sparkling water with ice and a slice of lemon to help herself feel as if it were a G and T. They had ordered food, Ava asking for a Caesar salad with potato wedges while Hazel declared she couldn't eat a bite but ordered salmon with thick cut chips just to keep Ava from feeling lonely.

'God, the last time I was pregnant they were still giving women Guinness to drink on the wards to help keep their iron levels up. There was a smoking room next to the nursery and they took the babies away at eight every evening and you didn't see them again until eight the next morning,' Hazel said sipping her faux G and T.

'You're in shock. You just need a bit of time to get used to the idea. It will be like riding a bike. You'll be fine.'

Hazel shot her a dirty look. 'That's easy for you to say. You've never had to push a nine-pound baby out your front jacksy.'

'You have to admit it *is* funny,' said Ava unable to resist giggling into her brandy glass.

'*Funny, funny*! You're not the one up the duff and nearly old enough to be a granny! There's nothing funny about it.'

'Come on now, you're only just turned forty-eight. Isn't it great that the pair of you still have it in you,' Ava said, trying to cajole Hazel into seeing the pregnancy in a more positive light.

'There's nothing wrong with my Robert, that's for sure, and there's me thinking I was menopausal. The doctor had a wee feel of my tummy, asked when I last had a period and sent me away to do a pee in a wee bottle. Jesus, I didn't think he would be calling me back to say I was with child.' She was smiling, her cheeks flushed with a mixture of pride and surprise.

'There you go. Sure, won't it be great having another wee Dale running around. It'll keep you young, so it will,' Ava said encouragingly.

'God, the thought of sleepless nights, dirty nappies, teething, and all that carry on, and here's me and Robert only starting to get used to having our independence and going away for holidays on our own.'

'But you'll have the boys to babysit and you're older and wiser. It'll be a breeze. To new beginnings.' Ava raised her glass and clinked it with Hazel's.

'New beginnings,' Hazel said, her eyes moist with happiness in spite of herself. 'I just hope Robert takes the news better than I did.'

Chapter 15

Scarlett threw her oversized tapestry holdall into the back of the taxi and told the driver to take her to ninety-seven Mount Pleasant Square, Malone Road, Belfast.

'You're not from round here with an accent like that, are you, love?' he asked as Scarlett reached across to fasten her seatbelt.

'No but I was born here. I've been away for quite a while. Over thirty years since I left and I haven't been back for nearly twenty-five.' She was self-conscious of her American accent, the upward inflection at the end of her sentences as if asking a question when making a simple statement. It was like a nervous tic. Maggie would have laughed at that and said it was all put on, in spite of the fact that Scarlett had spent more of her life in the US than in Ireland.

'You'll see some changes then. The bad days are long gone, thank God. The buck eejits that were busy blowing each other up twenty years ago spend their days sitting on committees up in Stormont now pushing bits of paper around, hob-nobbing with all the big wigs from across the water. Get invited to the White House every St Patrick's Day, so they do. No one thinks as to why they can't stay here and celebrate it in Ireland like with the rest of us.' He was on a roll, clearly glad to have a captive audience to listen to his take on Northern Irish politics.

'I bet the city has seen some changes. I hear there has been a lot of economic development — the peace dividend they were calling it in the US press,' Scarlett said, knowing taxi drivers the world over were the same, they all loved to talk about the state of the nation and how to put it right.

'Aye yer right there, that there has been. We've had a property boom like you won't believe but it's all going tits up now.

People got greedy and are sitting with negative equity on properties they can't sell or rent out for love nor money. Still, that's economics for you; highs and lows. Never had enough money myself to get burned in the gold rush, thank God. Something to be said for living hand to mouth. What you don't have, you can't lose,' he philosophised.

Scarlett put her head back on the headrest and shut her eyes, willing the driver to stop chatting. She was exhausted. The flight had been noisy with several young children taking it in turns to squawk or cry, their stressed-out parents doing all they could to settle them. She had tried to sleep on the flight, but every time she drifted off she had weird dreams about sinister black crows trying to peck at her hands. It left her feeling wary and anxious, and she couldn't shake off the feeling.

Now, she could hardly believe she was here. After all these years, she had done it. But what kind of reception would she get? Scarlett couldn't imagine being welcomed with open arms. That was way too much to expect. She was sure it would be slow and difficult at first but maybe, just maybe, she would be able to get to know the daughter she had left behind all those years earlier.

She would try to make Ava understand what it was like back then. How Belfast could choke the very life out of you, if you let it. Scarlett hadn't wanted to end up like Maggie, putting her days in with little more than a routine of cooking and washing up to do with only a TV set to distract her during her sessions with the mountain of ironing. A husband who was waited on hand and foot and never thought to say thanks. That was what she would have ended up with if she had stayed. She knew Johnny would have tried to be different, to give them a better life, but really after a while they would have ended up just like everyone else, small minded and *trapped*.

Scarlett had needed more. Did that make her a bad person? She thought she would implode in that little house. The humdrum existence threatened to smother her. Big ideas in a wee head were dangerous, her mother used to sagely say, much to Scarlett's annoyance. The express implication was that Scarlett wasn't to think beyond the four walls of Moonstone Street. She wasn't to dream of something different or better.

When she received the letter from her solicitor to say that ninety-seven Mount Pleasant Square had been signed over to Ava, she had felt something shift inside her. An awareness that time was finite. She couldn't hope that Ava would wait on her forever.

The taxi came to a stop. 'Here you are, love. That'll be twenty-two quid.'

Scarlett blinked awake. She must have dozed off. She glanced at the clock on the dashboard, nine thirty-five. Not too late to call unexpected. She fumbled in her big patchwork purse to find the cash to pay him. The taxi man opened the boot of his car and dragged out her holdall.

'Cheerio now, all the best. Have a good holiday!' he shouted as if they were old friends after a thirty-five-minute car ride.

She watched him drive away, still bleary eyed and tired, and then turned to look at the house and was shocked to see how run down it seemed. The hedging was so overgrown she had almost walked past the gate. Huge swaths of greenery spilled over onto the footpath. She picked up her holdall and opened the rusty clasp on the iron gate and began the walk up the driveway. It was so overgrown and broken up in places that it felt like she was undertaking a trek in the wilderness.

God, it was a dump. How could the house-proud Maggie have allowed the place to fall into such bad repair? Surely Ava would have been earning enough money to look after it and keep it in some sort of decent state?

By the time Scarlett reached the front door, she realised with a sinking heart that the house was empty. *Abandoned.*

The crumbling plaster on the bay windows, the peeling paint on the front door, and the cracked and broken terracotta pots on the front steps filled with nothing more than weeds, told her that she would find no one at home. Still, she couldn't help herself knocking, just in case. She lifted the heavy brass knocker, green and corroded with age, and banged it twice. It echoed in an obviously empty hallway. Throwing her bag over her shoulder she made her way round to the back of the house.

A large yellow skip, partially filled with old bits of wood, broken-up kitchen units and roof tiles sat squat on the driveway to the side of the house.

She came to a tall wooden locked gate but it was rotting away so she had no trouble pushing it open. Behind the gate she found that the garden was a thicket of overgrown shrubs and three-foot-tall weeds. The lawn had long since disappeared under the growth. In the dusky summer night, it looked wild and romantic, like a long forgotten secret garden waiting to be discovered.

Filled with curiosity, she peered into the window of the tall French doors and saw a ladder placed up against the far wall with some tools lying on the floor, a bucket and a trowel along with a half-used bag of plaster. Someone had started to fix up the place.

Scarlett had imagined many scenarios in her head on the flight over. She had visualised seeing Ava, a tall woman, her height a legacy from her father, with long flowing dark hair who would throw her arms open to embrace her long-lost mother. In other daydreams, she had pictured a resentful, surly girl not wanting to be won over by Scarlett's love for her. She would push her away, admonish her for her neglect. Full of fire and fight, not unlike a young Scarlett, and unwilling to hear her out.

But in all the possible set-ups she had envisaged, finding the house on Mount Pleasant Square derelict and empty had not been one of them.

What was she supposed to do now? It was getting dark, she had some money, but nowhere to go. She didn't fancy wandering around looking for a taxi and besides it was the eleventh night of July — bonfire night. The city would be full of drunks out celebrating, commemorating the Battle of the Boyne, though most of them didn't really care about King James and 1690, it was an excuse for tribal politicking and getting roaring drunk and sure if they came across a Catholic to give a kicking to well then it was all part of the cultural proceedings. It wouldn't be safe even in so called peacetime. Belfast was like any other city, give a thug a few beers and he would happily pick a fight without reason.

Besides, she was so tired. The journey had taken so much out of her. She tired easily these days. Her limitations were not what they used to be... *before.*

Without worrying about the consequences, she tried the handle of the French door. It was locked. Too bad. She moved on round to the back-kitchen door. It too was locked but she could see that the kitchen window latch was not firmly shut. The frame was practically rotting away. The house had really been left to fall down. It looked like no one had so much as given it a lick of paint in twenty-odd years. She gave the window frame a push but it didn't budge. She looked around the garden for something to poke the latch with. She found a stick and worked at the narrow gap in the window frame until she managed to lift up the latch, releasing the window and giving herself access. It wasn't too hard to throw in her bag and climb through, though she couldn't help feeling wary about going into an old empty house. It looked quite spooky in the gathering dusk. There could be dead bodies or anything lurking inside.

She braced herself and decided to trust her instincts. It was a good house with a sensitive soul which had been neglected for a very long time. It wouldn't do to make assumptions about bad things happening in it. There could be a million reasons why it was empty and not looked after.

Once inside, Scarlett had a look around. The house had definitely been empty for a long time. It smelt musty and neglected. The kitchen had been ripped out and the old cooker sat in the corner, unconnected, as if waiting to be carried out to the skip. The walls had been stripped of wallpaper so someone had been intending to renovate the place.

There was no fridge or washing machine and most of the walls looked like they needed plastering. There was sink and a cupboard still standing, over by the wall with the window.

She went on through to the living room. She tried the light switch but the electric was off, though she could still see around as it wasn't quite dark yet. An old blanket was spread out on the floor as if the house had been expecting a guest in need of somewhere to rest their head. She could make a bed for the night and then wonder what the hell to do the following day.

Ava had obviously moved on. Perhaps she was like Scarlett after all, a traveller who needed more than Belfast could offer. She could be halfway round the world, experiencing her own adventures.

Scarlett could remember the first day she saw number ninety-seven. She had been so full of herself back then. Thought that she could buy her child a secure happy home which wouldn't suffocate the life out of her. She had wandered around these rooms with the estate agent, a guy named Pete if she remembered correctly, who kept flirting with her, said he had recognised her immediately and asked if she would give him her autograph and her phone number. She had humoured him in the hope of getting the house off the market. She knew she wanted it and didn't want to get into a bidding war.

He had given the usual estate agent hard sell. Telling her all about the good schools close by, the parks and the prestigious BT9 postcode. All of it had meant little to Scarlett. She knew of the house. It was on her mother's cleaning rota. It belonged to a doctor and his family, the McCooleys. Maggie had always gone on about the grandeur of the place and how Mrs McCooley liked things just so. Scarlett had felt there was poetic justice in being able to buy it for her mother, the cleaner now living in the big house, as lady of the manor so to speak.

She could picture Maggie scrubbing the front steps and smugly sweeping up the leaves on the driveway, all the time feeling pride that she owned such a beautiful house. Scarlett knew only too well that Maggie was a humble woman of no pretension. But it would have been satisfying to think that she could have had enjoyed a lifestyle well beyond her normal means.

Of all the things Scarlett's fleeting success had brought her, money was not one she had much interest in. Being able to buy this house had felt like pay back to Maggie for looking after Ava. Her mother wasn't one for deep meaningful conversations. Scarlett could never have sat down with her and said how much she appreciated Maggie taking Ava on and giving her a good solid upbringing. As much as Scarlett resented the stifling atmosphere of Moonstone Street, she appreciated that a child need stability and routine. She could see for herself that Ava was a happy child who was doted on. So, buying number ninety-seven was the easiest way of saying thank you, while providing Ava with a wonderful house to grow up in. Something more than Scarlett had had. Perhaps having the luxury of such a house to grow in, a beautiful garden to play in, Ava could lose herself enough to never have to go looking for something else, just as Scarlett had to.

She put her hand on the pendant around her neck and rubbed it between her thumb and forefinger. She was wearing the necklace she had worn every day since the diagnosis, a rhodochrosite crystal, a pink, polished stone veined with luminous white streaks. A stone signifying strong bonds of love, with power to help remove blockages and strengthen emotional security. It was also believed to help ward off health problems concerning thyroid disorders and asthma. Even cancer.

Not that she truly believed such power. As far as Scarlett was concerned, the stones could help with emotional problems, provide a little lift in a life dogged by stress. Her clients came with problems of the self which only they could overcome, but sometimes believing in a higher power, or something outside of your control, could help just enough to move you forward beyond the clutches of whatever illness threatened.

She closed her eyes and tried to imagine Ava running around the rooms of the old house, at six, at ten, as a teenager. Whenever she envisaged her as a fully grown woman she could never put a face to the image. It was as if Ava as a young woman was always turning away, resisting meeting her mother's gaze.

And now here she was in Belfast, and it looked like Ava was long gone elsewhere.

Scarlett sat down on the tartan blanket and rummaged in her holdall for her toothbrush. When it came to packing up her life, she had very little to bring with her. She had sold off most of her belongings in a yard sale, and Stella had happily taken clothes and books. Scarlett's jewellery-making equipment would be sent on when she was more established and had discovered where she would be staying but for now, all that she needed was in the big tapestry bag she had bought for twelve dollars on a market stall.

She had nothing to eat but she wasn't hungry, just tired, bone tired. The next day she would call on the neighbours to see if they could help her track down Ava. Maybe they would be able to help her realign her compass and point herself towards her daughter.

Chapter 16

Ava turned over in her bed and tried to imagine what it would be like to never sleep in thirteen Moonstone Street again. She had organised a hire van and was going to move her few belongings into Mount Pleasant Square the following day. Ben and Daniel were going to do the heavy lifting. Niamh and Cal had intended to offer moral support and have a nosey round, but a work commitment in Dublin had prevented them from joining her. They couldn't wait to get nosing around and had already started discussing colour ways, fabric swatches and stainless-steel kitchen appliances as if they were her resident interior designers or 'abode stylists' as Cal kept saying.

The following day would be the twelfth of July bank holiday so they were all off work. While some of the country would be marching in their Orange bands, Ava and her friends would be busy hauling furniture about and stripping wallpaper if Ava could convince them that it was a fun way to spend their day. She would tell Cal next week it would be a stripping party rather than a painting party, and he might see the funny side and help out, as long as he didn't insist on being buck naked while he did it.

Ava had spent every spare weekend sanding down floors and sweeping up after the builders but had enjoyed every minute. Her evenings were still reserved for visiting Maggie. But it was amazing what a bit of clearing out and sweeping up had done to the place.

The garden was her next project to undertake. She was going to inquire if Quinn, the gardener at the Sisters of Mercy home, would be interested in earning a bit of extra money overhauling her wild garden. He seemed to be a nice fella. Quiet and kept to himself, but always tinkering about, mowing the lawns or cutting back shrubbery. She could ask Sister Lucy about him.

Ava pulled the duvet up over her head in an effort to get some sleep. The next day would be a busy day and she would need a good night's sleep.

Chapter 17

S carlett woke early with the morning sun warming her face, but was stiff and sore from sleeping on the hard floor. She arched her back to relieve the stiffness and stood up to stretch her aching joints. The long flight, and the disappointment of finding the house empty and neglected, had taken its toll on her. She felt like crying but managed to pull herself together. A new day might bring some fresh information and explain all of this.

She padded towards the back of the house to find the kitchen in search of something to drink, hoping the tap was still connected to the water supply. Her mouth was dry and her throat was scratchy-sore. In the bright morning light, she realised that there was another room to the left of the kitchen which she had missed the previous night. It looked like someone had decided to resituate the kitchen in what would have been the old morning room. In the newly appointed kitchen she found it had been fitted out with smart white cupboards and a shiny grey granite work surface.

She found an old chipped cup sitting on the stainless-steel drainer and let the tap run for a few minutes before filling it with chilly cold water. It seemed that the house was being overhauled. It could be that Ava had decided to do it up, with the intention of putting it up for sale. Either that or she had already sold it and the new buyers would be horrified to find Scarlett squatting overnight. She assumed Moonstone had long since been sold.

Curious now, she made her way around the downstairs rooms. The main drawing room had been freshly plastered. The walls, still drying out, were a shade of soft pinky grey. Light flooded in from the large bay window, making the room inviting and warm.

It would be lovely when it was finished, she thought. The other downstairs rooms were in varying stages of work. The hallway still had the original wallpaper although someone had begun stripping it, leaving crumbling plaster beneath the areas exposed.

She climbed the stairs, her bare feet cautiously avoiding pieces of chipped plaster and the odd nail. Upstairs was much the same — a work in progress. She found the main bathroom and freshened up. She was glad to have a wee and to be able to wash her face even though the water was freezing.

She was cross with herself for not having written to Ava before arriving unannounced. There had been many times over the years she had sat down trying to compose a letter, but had always abandoned it, failing to put into words how she felt and how desperately regretful she was that they hadn't maintained contact. Then, when she was diagnosed with cancer, she felt that she had no right to expect any reconciliation.

The splash of cold water had refreshed her, making her feel suddenly wide-awake yet ravenous. She felt a renewed optimism that she would track Ava down. She would knock on the neighbouring house and ask if they knew of Ava, and perhaps they would know how she could contact her. Trouble was, with it being the twelfth of July, many people would be away on holiday. The shops and cafes might be closed too so she would have to find herself a B&B to stay in and get something to eat.

She dried her face off on the end of her crinkled skirt and headed out onto the landing to pack up her tapestry holdall and begin looking for Ava. But before she had chance to put her foot on the first step of the creaky threadbare carpeted stairs, she heard voices outside and a key turning in the lock of the front door.

*

Ava took one last look around thirteen Moonstone Street. To all intents and purposes, the living room looked exactly the same as it always had. The sofa was well worn, yet comfortable, the gold and green floral curtains were pulled wide open to let in the early morning sunlight, Maggie's ornaments and clock standing on top of the fireplace, and the television, a black box of silence, sat still in the corner. She'd spent hours sitting at the table playing cards or board games with Joseph or doing her homework.

Nothing had changed and yet, it could never be the same.

Most of Ava's possessions were packed up in boxes, stacked in the hall, waiting to be lifted, and put into the rented white van. She had cleared out her bedroom, deciding to take her little, neat single bed with her, and her books, along with her small television which Maggie had bought her many Christmases earlier. Her clothes, handbags and her shoes and boots were packed into two suitcases. She had used the move as an opportunity to have a good clear-out, and under Niamh's watchful eye had culled all items of clothing which looked dated or shabby. The end result being that Ava no longer had much to wear. Still, Niamh was right, she needed a revamp and for once she was open to the idea.

The short beep of a horn from the van outside interrupted her thoughts. 'Right,' she said to herself, 'this is it,' and she closed the living room door ready to make her move into ninety-seven Mount Pleasant Square.

Ben climbed down out of the hired van and gave Ava a quick hug and a kiss.

'So, you're definitely moving?' he asked half joking. Ava had spent many evenings listing the pros and cons of the move, debating whether or not it was wrong to leave Moonstone Street while Maggie was so unwell and unable to voice her opinion on the matter. He had listened patiently and then told Ava that he couldn't advise her what to do, sure didn't he still live with his parents? She chuckled at that and was reminded once again of how slow she had been to venture beyond her own safe little nest.

'We'll put the bed in first and then stack the boxes around it,' said Ben sounding like he knew what he was talking about.

His brother Daniel climbed out of the white van looking hung-over.

'Heavy night?' asked Ava.

He closed his eyes against the bright sunlight and circled his shoulders as if loosening up in preparation for the heavy lifting. 'I think it must have been. My head is pounding.'

'Sure, a bit of exercise will do you good,' joked Ava. She had come to like Daniel and his easy-going ways over the last while. He had met her and Ben for drinks a couple of times and was always good company and had so far maintained his promise not to let on to Hazel about her and Ben.

When they had the van fully packed and the last of the boxes loaded, Ava shut the front door. She stood back and looked at the wee two-up two-down house, and felt tears threaten to well up. She was being silly really, since it wouldn't be the last time she was here. She wasn't selling Moonstone Street, so she could always pop back when she wanted to, but she knew, deep down, it would never feel the same again.

Since Maggie had moved in with the Sisters of Mercy, the house had felt less like home anyhow. It was time to move on and embrace a new stage in her life. She had spent too long letting life happen to other people. It was her turn to engage in a bit of excitement. Breaking up with Finlay had been the instigation she needed.

'Ready?' asked Ben from the driver's seat.

'Sure, it's now or never.' Ava climbed up into the van, fastened her seat belt and braced herself for a new direction.

*

'Lift it higher and grab the end, will you? I seem to be getting all the weight!' Ben shouted to Daniel as they tried to manoeuvre the single bed through the front door of Mount Pleasant Square.

'I've got the bloody end!' Daniel shouted back.

Ava came behind them carrying the first of the many boxes. 'Keep the noise down would you. I don't want the neighbours thinking badly of me and I haven't even moved in yet. If I had known you two were going to behave like the Chuckle Brothers I would have hired a real removal firm,' she said, setting the box down in the hallway. 'Up the stairs and first room on the right.'

She turned sharply as something caught her eye. There, in the corner of the drawing room, she saw a bag. She walked in to look at it. A large tapestry carpetbag which didn't belong to her and certainly didn't look like something any of the work men would have owned, was sitting, wide open. She crossed the drawing room and picked up the bag. It was heavy and seemed full, packed to capacity. She was almost fearful of something jumping out at her, practical joke style. Inside she saw clothes: lots of silky kimono-style tops and comfortable looking wide leg trousers, a few long cotton skirts, the type of clothes you would describe as hippy. She rummaged further down and felt a soft leather purse. As she pulled it out for inspection, she could hear the footsteps of Ben and Daniel overhead as they placed the single bed in the master bedroom.

When she unbuttoned the silver-grey leather purse and examined a Visa debit card, she felt the fine hairs on the back of her neck stand up. There, on the plastic cards in embossed print, she read: Scarlett Mary Connors. *Her mother.*

Ava's mind tried to grasp hold of the information. She was sitting in Mount Pleasant Square with Scarlett's bag at her knees, looking through her clothes and personal belongings and staring at the name Scarlett Mary Connors.

Ava was snapped out of her reverie by the pounding of Ben and Daniel on the stairs. She jumped up and walked out to the hallway, leaving the bag where she'd found it.

'Right that's the bed and the chair in. We only have a few boxes left. This house is so big your stuff has just been swallowed up,' said Daniel.

'I know,' Ava said, 'it will take me years to furnish it. Just throw the boxes into the hall, and you two can head off. I'm sure your mum has a barbeque or something planned.' She wanted them to leave so she could find Scarlett. She had to be in the house somewhere.

Ben gave her a kiss. 'You sure you don't want a hand unpacking?' He was like a puppy dog always seeking affection and reassurance.

'No honestly, you've done enough. I'll give you a call later on in the week.' She waved them off and closed the door, wondering what on earth Scarlett was doing back again, and where she was hiding.

Chapter 18

Ava had yearned to reconnect with Scarlett for so long. God, the nights Ava had spent in Moonstone Street, dreaming of her mother and imagining all sorts of wild adventures. Would she be at some glamorous party full of Hollywood film stars or would she be singing and playing guitar with her band, entertaining her adoring fans? Maybe she was thinking about Ava at exactly the same moment. Ava would squeeze her eyes shut and concentrate on sending a telepathic message to wherever she was.

Mum, it's me, Ava. I love you, come and visit me soon.

Growing up without a mother wasn't always hard. Maggie had made sure Ava was not short of love or attention, but there had been moments when she knew that no matter how good Maggie was, there was always that sense of someone missing.

Many nights lying in that little room in Moonstone Street, when she couldn't find sleep, she climbed out of bed and opened the dark oak door of her wardrobe. There, at the very back behind the shoes, the boots and the handbags, she would drag out an old duffle bag. Over time it had faded from purple to a soft shade of heather.

It used to hold a lingering scent of Scarlett's musk and patchouli oil perfume, but over time it smelt of nothing more than dust and memories. Reaching into it, she rummaged past the pastel-coloured envelopes holding the never posted letters from her childhood and teenage years. They were toe-curling, embarrassing letters she had written to her mother, detailing all her problems, worries and hopes for the future.

She pulled out a photograph, three inches by three inches square, faded with age – Scarlett standing in a field, her jeans bleached pale blue, worn tight and flared at the bottom. Her hair hung in two long silky, dark brown plaits and she beamed out at Ava, her eyes screwed up against the glare of the sun.

Next, she dragged out the long woollen scarf, knitted in loose stitches of violets, blues and soft pinks. Ava wrapped it around her neck just as she used to do when she was small; trying to imagine Scarlett's embrace. Ava sat on her knees picturing her mother's comforting love. Just like she used to do when school was hard, when she had fought over something silly with Niamh, when Maggie had scolded her and sent her to her room.

At the bottom of the bag there lay a silver locket, tarnished with age. Ava opened the catch and looked at the tiny photograph of herself as a baby in her mother's arms. While it was difficult to remember Scarlett, her fleeting visits stopped early on, she could almost imagine what it was like to be held by her, rocked in her mother's arms. Imagination was a fine thing she thought, sniffing. God, if Maggie knew how she had been maudlin over Scarlett's old cast-off bag of trinkets and memories, she would have told her to wash her face and quit feeling miserable.

Now, there she was standing on the landing of Mount Pleasant Square about to come face to face with Scarlett. Ava's heart felt fit to burst.

The door of the bathroom opened and there she stood. There was no mistaking her. Shoulder-length chestnut brown hair falling into loose unkempt waves. Her eyes blinking, wide and bright, from beneath a fringe, staring in wonder. They looked at each other, uncertain and fearful. Neither wanting to make the first move, and then Scarlett, as if realising that it was indeed Ava standing before her, reached out and gently put her hand on Ava's arm. It seemed as though she was making sure Ava was real and not an apparition.

'Ava, is it you?' she asked, her American accent echoing in the old bathroom.

'Yes. You're here,' Ava said — her voice flat and quiet. She didn't know how to react. Was she supposed to welcome her with joy, or to cautiously sound her out first? It was like looking at a stranger. But then again, that was exactly what they were to each other; strangers, connected by blood ties and a shared family history, but really, they knew nothing of each other.

Ava was struck by how delicate and thin Scarlett was. Her face was aged and lined but not overly so. She looked well. Her clothes were gypsy-like; a long floaty skirt, in shades of taupe and coffee, wore with a sheer-cotton cream blouse with billowing sleeves and a ruffled collar. Around her neck she wore an unusual, plaited gold chain with a heavy looking glossy, pink stone hanging from it, which her hand had grabbed hold of as if for comfort or reassurance.

They stood for a few seconds, taking each other in. Neither knowing what to say. Scarlett took a step back and leaned against the tiled wall, the grout looking distinctively grotty.

'What happened? To the house I mean, it's falling down,' Scarlett said.

Ava shrugged and cringed inwardly. What a thing to say. Her first words to her long-lost daughter where an admonishment, as if it were all her fault that the house was run down.

'I've only just moved in today. It's going to take a long time to make it nice, but I don't mind making do, and living here while all the work goes on. Besides, the messier jobs have been finished and the kitchen is fitted out.'

It didn't seem right to be standing in the old cold bathroom talking about the house. It was her mother, her long-lost mother, standing right there in front of her. Surely, they should be some sort of fanfare, clasping hugs and tears at least.

Ava moved awkwardly towards Scarlett to give her a handshake or a hug, she didn't know which was required, and opted for a sort of pat on her arm instead. 'So here you are.'

'Yeah, at long last. Here I am. I suppose we have a bit of catching up to do.' Scarlett smiled as if to make light of the fact that she had been absent without leave for twenty-five years.

Chapter 19

Meeting Finlay had been the last thing on Ava's mind when she settled into the soft tobacco-coloured leather sofa in The Dirty Onion bar. Ben had persuaded her to go out for a drink and she had agreed, knowing she wasn't likely to run into Hazel at a student bar in Belfast. She was still wary of Hazel finding out that she was messing around with her son. Once the trauma of the necklace in the bed episode had passed, Ava had come around to dating Ben in an *unofficial* capacity. She told him it was to be on a need-to-know basis and he was certainly not to go telling his mates for fear of word getting back to his mother. Hazel and Robert had enough going on with the late pregnancy.

A quick drink in a student bar qualified as a date. They had been to the cinema a few times and had attended one of Niamh's wrap parties, but mostly they just hung out at Mount Pleasant Square.

Ava had to admit Ben was fun to be around. He didn't let anything hassle him, he talked about his coursework at the University of Ulster and his plans to set up his own software company, specialising in alarm systems. He never pressured her or expected anything from her. They just seemed to enjoy each other's company.

And the sex was great. Really great.

Ava had to admit that with Ben it was different. She was under no illusions that it was down to Ben's sexual prowess. Technically he hadn't done anything that Finlay hadn't done, nor was he physically better; it was more a case of Ava having awoken her sexual side. She was more willing to lose herself in the moment and let the pleasure wash over her in little shudders of pure ecstasy — something which hadn't happened with Finlay. Sex with Finlay had been controlled, methodical and lovely. But with Ben it was fast, hot and scorching. God, she had friction burns to prove it. She felt her face flush hot just thinking about it, and then shame tormented her again as she thought of Hazel, and how she would feel if she found out. But thankfully, the chances of Hazel popping in for a drink in a student dive like The Dirty Onion were slim.

Besides, Hazel had other plans that night. She and Robert were having their first antenatal birthing class. Ava and Hazel had both sniggered over their sandwiches at lunchtime at the thought of poor Robert being dragged along to talk about all the squeamish bits he had so safely avoided the first three times round. Hazel had told Ava how he had phoned the hospital during her epically long labour with Ross to leave a message saying: 'Good luck, love. Hope all goes well. I'm thinking about you.'

He wasn't getting off so lightly this time. Hazel had gone all new age and was looking into waterbeds, reflexology and hypnotherapy as pain management alternatives. She had even read up on orgasmic birthing but told Ava she had dismissed the idea as she didn't like the thought of it. If all the alternative therapy stuff failed, Robert had the express instructions to ensure she was given an epidural. Pronto.

All of this was racing through Ava's head when she glanced up at the door and saw Finlay Kane walking in with his hand holding onto Rose's. Ava felt like crawling under the table and hiding. It was too late and too obvious to do anything but rearrange her features from shock to pleasantly surprised and hope he hadn't registered the fleeting expression of pure heart-breaking longing.

God, he looked so good, she thought, wishing she had a drink to stop her mouth going dry. How had she forgotten to notice just how gorgeous he was? She must have been in a coma for the last eight years to not have been panting for him. He strode over to her in six quick footsteps, Rose trailing behind him.

'Ava, hi,' he said, planting a warm kiss on her cheek. 'I hardly recognised you with the new hair colour. It suits you.' He smelt of bonfires on beaches and late summer nights.

She kept forgetting how different it was to other people and self-consciously put her hand to hair.

'I haven't seen you about for a while. How are you keeping?' he asked, his low voice affecting her in ways it never had before.

'Fine, good,' she managed to say, her mouth suddenly sandpaper dry.

He squeezed past the table beside her and sat down close enough for her to reach out and touch him if she so desired, while Rose took the seat opposite.

'Sorry, I'm a complete eejit. Ava this is Rose. Rose this is Ava,' he said, clearly delighted with himself as if he had just reunited two long-lost sisters.

'Hiya, Ava. I've heard all about you. Good to meet you.' She held out her thin, delicate, neatly manicured hand which Ava accepted, noticing the soft shell-pink nail varnish and the fine silver chain bracelet on Rose's wrist. She was suddenly embarrassed by her own coarse, rough skin and ragged, short nails courtesy of working in a florist for years.

Ava noted how Rose's blue eyes ran over Ava's clothes as if taking an itinerary of her casual, slightly scruffy outfit. She wished she had worn the new skinny jeans and sparkly blouse she had left hanging in her wardrobe. Instead she was in the same old shapeless jeans she always wore to work, with a purple silk top. Nothing special and only one step up from the dark green fleece, embroidered with Blooming Dale's Floristry on the breast pocket, that she had been wearing an hour before. Humiliating.

She felt a jealous irritation at the sight of Rose's beautifully, put together outfit: a little, tight fitting grey cardigan over a sharp, smart white shirt of which the first three buttons were left casually opened to relieve her neat, honey-coloured cleavage, while her long legs were clad in sharp pinstriped grey trousers. Classy and professional, yet oh-so-sexy. Her blonde hair was tied back in a low ponytail, with just enough swish to look cute and girly. How could Finlay resist? She was everything Ava wasn't. Polished and done to perfection. Ava could imagine Rose would make the perfect blushing bride and then the ideal mother Finlay so clearly longed for.

Just then, Ben arrived back from the bar clutching two bottles of Budweiser. God, she was going to look like a complete loser, drinking Bud from a bottle instead of sophisticated and elegant sipping from a chilled glass of white wine.

'Hi there. Finlay, isn't it?' Ben asked setting the drinks down.

'Aye, how are you? You're Hazel's son, right?' Finlay had met Ben on a few occasions in passing at the shop.

'Yeah,' said Ben putting his arm casually around Ava's shoulders as if to mark his territory, both annoying and pleasing Ava, all at once. She noted the surprise on Finlay's face. He raised his eyebrows slightly and looked at her pointedly, as if to say, *really?*

Ava turned her face up to Ben, smiling. *That'll show him*, she thought. *Two can play at that game.* But really, she knew it wasn't her style to play games at all. She just wanted to have her pride restored, and if being on Ben's arm did that, then so be it.

Ben and Finlay had begun exchanging football information, boring stats that men called to mind whenever they needed to create a conversation. *Before we know it, they'll be discussing fuel prices and comparing engine sizes*, Ava thought as she put the cold beer bottle to her lips and sipped her drink as delicately as she could. Rose looked at Ava expectantly as if waiting on her to initiate a conversation. Good manners prevented Ava from dismissing her with a curt smile.

'So, Rose, have you and Finlay been going out together for long?' Ava asked as a conversation starter.

'It's our six-week anniversary actually,' she said a touch too smugly while smiling sweetly. 'I know you two went out for... what was it? Eight years? But I suppose it was one of those relationships that dragged on without meaning to,' she added, her nude-coloured lipstick slick lips pressed into a thin smile to disguise the nasty barbed comment. She turned towards Finlay, laying a proprietorial hand on his arm.

Ava was relieved to see Finlay standing up. 'Right, I'll leave you two to it, and go get us a drink at the bar. Nice seeing you again, Ava. I'll give you a call and we can get together for a proper catch up.' He looked directly into her eyes and she could have sworn she had seen something flicker, regret maybe or perhaps it was regret that he had wasted so much time in a relationship that had dragged on without meaning to.

'Sure, that would be nice,' she replied, throwing Rose a sweet smile.

Chapter 20

'What did you make of the class?' Ava asked Hazel over their usual lunch of sandwiches and tea. They were sitting out the back of the shop, glad of a quiet half hour. Hazel's ankles looked like they had been pumped up and she was feeling the strain of standing behind the counter even if she only did a few hours a day.

'Oh, it was a hoot. There's me thinking I would be as old as Methuselah waddling in with my big bump and didn't I find that most of them were in their late thirties and two of them were even forty plus. Apparently, all the career women are waiting much longer these days before having their first, so there's hope for you yet,' Hazel said, elbowing Ava in the ribs, before breaking her ciabatta roll into two and beginning to demolish it. She was constantly complaining of being hungry these days. 'Mind you, the antenatal teacher said if you go to the NHS classes, it's a different story. Wee girls as young as fifteen sitting snivelling into their hankies as the realisation of what they have let themselves in for sinks in. The teacher had this plastic pelvis and a doll to demonstrate the birth, and she told us how one wee girl had fainted clean away. Just passed out cold at the thought of it. Mind you, every time someone mentions ten centimetres dilated, it near enough takes my breath away. First time round I knew nothing until it was too late to back out. Ignorance is bliss as they say.'

'And what did Robert make of it? Did he let you down by being all squeamish?'

'Oh no, he sat there as proud as a peacock. Thinks he's like Brad Pitt with all those children running around. The teacher suggested that in the third trimester our partners massage our perineum with oil, and yer man wanted to know did he have to wait till then! I tell ye it has certainly put a spark back into things, if you know what I mean.'

'Oh, please spare me the details. I don't want to know what goes on in your bedroom and you a pregnant woman and all!' Ava laughed. Hazel was certainly blooming. She had ensured that she had plenty of rest periods and indulged in regular "with child" spa treatments. All for the well-being of the baby, she claimed.

'And the boys have been great. Making a real effort about the house and bringing me cups of raspberry leaf tea. Ben is moving out; did I tell you?'

'Yeah, you mentioned it. I thought you always said you'd be suicidal when the time came for your boys to leave home,' said Ava.

'I know. I thought it would be really hard to let them go but you know what? It just feels that the time has come and sure my wee nest won't be empty for long,' she stroked her bump proudly. 'I'm just relieved that Mickey's off the scene. Apparently, Ben was seeing someone else, a mystery girl, and Mickey got wind of it and gave him his marching orders. Good riddance, I say,' she said, refilling her cup with tea. 'So, the plan is to decorate Ben's room as the nursery though we haven't a clue what colour to paint it. Robert says he's holding off until we have the scan and can find out the sex to know what colour to paint it. But I'm not so sure I want to know. I kind of like the suspense. Can you imagine me with a wee girl after three boys? I'd go pink mad. But sure, you get what you get and I'll be happy no matter what.'

'Any name yet?' asked Ava, wanting to move the subject away from Ben but knowing fine well that Hazel would be changing her mind right up to the birth date.

'At the minute, it's Brodie Lauren for a girl and Nathan Kyle for a boy, but don't hold me to them I know I'll probably change my mind when I see him or her. Our Daniel was called Simon for five days but everyone kept joking saying where's wee Simple Simon. I couldn't be having that, so I went with Daniel instead and as soon as I called him Daniel, he turned his wee head as if to say, yes, that's my name.'

Ava still blushed when Ben's name came up in conversation with Hazel. Her conscience prickled with discomfort. At times she tried to belittle her relationship, putting it down to a harmless fling, but then she didn't want to risk hurting Hazel or Ben so why did she allow it to go on? It was time to call it a day and to finish with Ben for good. He would be back on the club scene by the weekend picking up some wee girl closer in age to himself and a whole lot more suitable.

'So, tell me all about Scarlett then,' said Hazel rinsing out her cup at the sink.

'Sure, I've told you everything. There she was, trying to track me down and thought I had spent my childhood being brought up in Mount Pleasant Square, instead of the little house on Moonstone Street. She near had the shock of her life when she heard the removal men deliver my bed and stuff.'

'How did you get removal men to work on the twelfth, it's a bank holiday?'

Ava swallowed the last of her chicken tikka salad sandwich. 'West Belfast firm, sure they're not gonna take the twelfth off.' She wasn't ready to confess that Ben had been the chief removal man.

'And did Scarlett just arrive, like, with no warning?'

'Yes, packed up her stuff and headed for Belfast, expecting to find me in mourning for Maggie. When she had been notified that the house had been signed over to me, she assumed that it was because Maggie had died. I don't know if she was more surprised to find out she was alive and in the Sisters of Mercy home, or that I had only just discovered Mount Pleasant Square.' Ava had to admit it was all a bit unsettling. At first, she assumed Scarlett would want to have the Mount Pleasant house back, but she was adamant that it was always meant to be for Ava. It was where Scarlett had pictured Ava growing up.

When she had initially filled in Hazel all about Scarlett, she had sat wide-eyed in wonder. Ava knew that Hazel couldn't fathom how a mother could have absconded, never mind how Ava could welcome her into her life so readily. It was clear Hazel was itching to see Mount Pleasant Square and meet Scarlett. But Ava had told her to bide her time. She needed to sort it all out, before she began introducing her long-lost mother to her friends. One step at a time.

She didn't want Hazel to see the house until it was more presentable. At the minute, the sash windows were being sanded down in preparation for being painted, the heating was still on the blink and the kitchen and bathrooms were no more than works in progress. But still, Ava loved it. She had swept and cleaned every inch of the beautiful old wood block floors, and then on her hands and knees rubbed beeswax into the grain, bringing out the reddish-brown mahogany colour. The walls may have been crumbling in places and damp lurking in a couple of corners, but the high ceilings and wide doorways made it feel airy and bright.

Hazel couldn't be put off forever. Her inherent nosiness meant that she would nag away at Ava until she gave in and introduced her to Scarlett and let her have a guided tour of Mount Pleasant Square. Hopefully it would be when Ben was safely tucked out of the way.

Chapter 21

'Haven't seen you for a while. Been busy, have you?' The voice came from deep down in the sunken glen of the tropical ravine house in the Botanic Gardens.

It was funny that the one place Ava loved to come to clear her thoughts had been the one she had been avoiding for weeks. Her head was all over the place and she didn't think sitting amongst the plants would help. Maybe she had been wrong.

It was Marvin, the botanist. He was working with a tall flowering vine which reached as far as the high glass ceiling, coming back down on itself, when it found it had nowhere else to go.

'Yes, it's been non-stop this last while. How about you? Keeping busy in here?' Ava replied, looking down on him from the iron walk way which ran around the artificially created glen, basically a basement carved out of the earth below providing the height necessary for the collection of rainforest plants and trees to grow. She leaned over on the waist high cast iron railing to watch him working below her.

'Same as usual. Always something to be done. Come on down and have a look at this.'

Ava had never been down into the heart of the ravine before; it was strictly for staff with visitors being confined to the walkway above. She left her handbag hanging on the railing and climbed down the ladder towards Marvin.

'What do you think this is?' He gently squeezed one of the shiny, green, leathery leaves releasing its scent.

'Oh, I don't know.' She touched the plant's pale parchment-like bark. 'It smells like a damp mildew Christmas cake. Mmm, I'm not sure... Is it cloves?'

'Nope. It's cinnamon. At harvest time, the rough bark on the outside is removed and beaten to soften it, so that it peels away in strips. Then the strips are laid out in overlapping layers and rolled up into quills to be sun-dried, giving us cinnamon as we know it.' He clearly loved showing off his vast knowledge of the plants he tended.

'Have a wander round down here if you like, just don't let on to anyone,' Marvin said, his big doughy, soft face smiling widely.

Ava thanked him and let her mind drift as she looked at the plant life all around her. There was something therapeutic about caressing the bark, the stems, and the huge oversized leaves. It felt like she had been shrunk down to a Borrower-sized person and that she was trekking around in a gigantic greenhouse, that or she had been dropped into a rain forest but the absence of snakes and creepy crawlies made it feel like a sanitised version.

Huge lush leaves brushed against her face as she strolled around, sweeping away the worry and doubts which had been niggling away at her for weeks. She could barely keep up with her thoughts, one-minute thinking of Finlay and the next worrying about Maggie, and then trying to fit Scarlett into the picture.

Memories of being with Finlay kept haunting her. She thought of the little holidays they had taken: a weekend in Donegal in a croft advertised as the 'true spirit of the north west of Ireland'. They had turned up to find they were staying in a hovel with its dirt floors covered with rugs. It was the type of old place that housed the farm animals downstairs at night time to provide extra heat for the family sleeping over head in the loft like ledge. They had looked around horrified but then resolved to make the best of it. The cooking took place over a big open turf fire and they had to use an outside loo. But she had beautiful memories of lying in front of the fire, her skin warmed by the sparking and burning turf, as Finlay had explored every part of her body with a gentle tenderness.

Then there was the time they had broken down on the way to Antrim. A day out to visit Finlay's sister had turned into a complete nightmare as they were stranded waiting for a tow truck to come and bring them back to Belfast. It had been snowing heavily and the whole world seemed to have been blanketed in the hush of snow. They were cold and bored waiting but, somehow, they had made the best of the situation and had cuddled up for warmth. The AA man wrapped on the steamed-up window and interrupted their passionate snogging session, leaving red faces all round. She couldn't help smile at the memory, thinking of Finlay hastily jumping out of the car.

Now she couldn't help wonder how he was. What he was doing, and more importantly, who he was doing it with. As lovely as Ben was, he didn't measure up to Finlay, and Ava could hardly believe that she had allowed herself to drift through the years with him without realising just how special he was. But she knew she had missed her chance. It was time she moved on. Life wasn't for living in the past with memories for comfort.

She buried her nose in a particularly beautiful orange flower, enjoying the warm musky scent. Maggie was her other worry. She had been sleeping a lot and appeared to be less aware of everything around her. Sister Lucy had tried to reassure Ava, telling her that sometimes the body needs to withdraw to heal, but Ava was concerned that there was something seriously wrong. The GP had checked on her and was satisfied that her blood pressure, heartbeat and temperature were all normal. Ava could hardly push for more tests when it appeared Maggie was fine. It was just so hard to watch her decline. It was as if she was shutting down ready to move on to whatever afterlife might have to offer.

When Ava had taken Scarlett to see Maggie for the first time at the Sisters of Mercy home she had hoped that Maggie would be pleased or at least show some reaction. But she had been sleeping and they didn't want to disturb her seemingly peaceful slumber. 'Never worry,' Scarlett had said. 'There'll be other days to visit and reacquaint ourselves.'

Ava could see something like relief pass over Scarlett's face. She had been visibly shocked to see how old and frail Maggie looked but then joked on the way home that she looked great for a corpse.

'At least I'll have time to make amends with Mum,' Scarlett said, looking at Ava. 'I didn't think I'd get that chance.'

Ava was thrilled to see them together. She still felt like pinching herself every time she caught sight of Scarlett. Her real mum. Actually here, in the flesh. Not dreamt up in some childish fantasy while lying in her bed in Moonstone Street.

In all the years Ava had thought of her reunion with Scarlett, she had never really dwelled on what it might mean for Maggie to find her long-lost daughter. Maybe it was just what she needed to make her well again.

Chapter 22

The next day, Ava went shopping with Niamh. Window-shopping, for interior ideas in the ridiculously expensive shops along the Lisburn Road.

'Now remember, we are only here for inspiration. You can look and you can touch, but you most certainly cannot buy,' said Niamh as they made their way into Beaufort Interiors.

'God, it even smells expensive never mind how it all looks,' whispered Ava, her eyes wide taking it all in.

'It is. So, don't even ask the price of anything. We'll get ideas and do it on a shoestring budget. Cal is a dab hand with a piece of fabric and a glue gun. So, we are here for referencing only.' Niamh took the lead and strolled around the plush interior. A champagne-gold chaise longue dominated the first setting with brocade and tasselled cushions placed just so. Ornate marble inset lamps stood on either side of a huge mahogany sideboard while a gold scrolled mirror hung on the wall.

'Please tell me this isn't to your taste,' hissed Ava.

'Don't worry, I won't get carried away. Just try to visualise accents of gold in a cream palate. Take little hints of what they are doing and translate to a more liveable setting,' said Niamh, sounding like she knew what she was talking about.

'I'm not seeing it,' said Ava fingering the gold lamé tassels.

Niamh snatched her hand away. 'Come on let's have a look down the back.'

They made their way through the store, oohing and ahhing as they touched sumptuous fabrics and looked at interesting objet d'arts.

'Niamh, look at this,' Ava said as she sat tentatively on a gorgeous cream calfskin sofa. 'Feel it. It's as soft as a baby's bum.'

'Oh, it's lovely,' said Niamh, stroking the soft leather.

'I couldn't afford this in a million years and even if I could, I don't think I'd ever let anyone sit on it for fear of destroying it.'

'Can I help you, ladies?' a tall weedy man asked as he straightened the cushions proprietorially.

'We're just looking, thanks,' said Niamh, determined not to be intimidated by a bossy shop assistant.

They finished their wander round the shop and decided to treat themselves to a coffee in the nearby café.

'I was wanting to talk to you about something,' Niamh said lighting up a cigarette.

'What's up?'

She blew out a plume of smoke. 'I'm thinking of moving to London.'

'You're what? Why?' Ava asked, horrified at the thought of losing her best friend.

'I'm fed up with it here. Same jobs on short contracts, same clubs and pubs, always bumping into the same people every week. I need to make a change.'

'Is this about Colm Ferguson?'

'No. Yes. Partly. It's just — now don't laugh — I feel like I've had all the decent fellas over here. They're not so hot and I can't keep hoping the next married man will leave his wife. Not that I really want them to. Oh, it's just complicated.'

Ava put her hand on top of Niamh's. 'Honey don't go running away. I know that there is someone out there for you. Please don't move. What would me and Cal do without you? I'd end up going back to my old ways with mousy brown hair and bad clothes, looking like Ugly Betty.'

Niamh smiled. 'Nothing's decided yet. But I'm just going to put out some feelers for work, see if there is anything going. I'm contracted to do that film with Liam Neeson up in Draperstown for twelve weeks, so it's not as if I'm about to hop on a plane and disappear. If I do go it would need to be thought out and planned properly.'

'Your mum and dad would be devastated,' Ava reasoned.

'Sure, they could come over and see all the West End shows. It isn't as if I'm talking about going to Australia.'

Ava sipped her latte. She would hate to see Niamh leave, but she understood that Niamh needed something more than what Belfast had to offer.

Chapter 23

For a house in the middle of renovation, Ava had managed to create little rooms of habitable space. She had set up a makeshift dining room off the kitchen, with a cream lace tablecloth, taken from Maggie's airing cupboard, placed over an old wallpapering table. With candles and a jam jar filled with wildflowers from the garden, it looked inviting. Scarlett was coming around for dinner, and Ava wanted to make her feel welcome.

At times, she could hardly believe that Scarlett was back in her life. It was as if Mount Pleasant Square had magically summoned her up. Initially, they were polite and distant, sort of feeling each other out and taking it easy. They spent time with Maggie and had coffee together or went for walks along the River Lagan.

But now, they were more relaxed in each other's company, and over a Chinese takeaway meal and a bottle of red wine, followed by Copeland gin and tonics, they set about putting the world to rights.

'Sometimes you have to lose yourself before you find yourself, before you find real love,' Scarlett said trying not to miss her mouth as she brought the glass up towards her lips.

'Jesus that's desperate,' snorted Ava into her drink. 'You've definitely been in America way too long.'

For some reason, that cracked the two of them up. They hooted as if it were the funniest thing they had ever heard.

'Oh, don't, I'm going to wet myself,' giggled Ava. She couldn't believe how they were getting on. It was like finding a sister, a friend and a mother all rolled into one.

'So seriously then, tell me – Ben, is he *significant?*' Scarlett asked, lying back on the blanket.

Ava put her head down on the blanket. Scarlett's American accent was the only thing that seemed alien to Ava. Her hands, the tilt of her head, her stubby toes all seemed so familiar.

'God, no. Ben... well, Ben has been lovely. Really lovely. He is easy on the eye, gentle when it matters, but I'm nearly ten years older than him, for God's sake. I can't see that working out, and besides, if his mother finds out she's likely to kill me. You might find me impaled on a sycamore tree in the middle of Botanic Avenue.'

'You might be surprised. His mother might think you are just the woman he needs to calm him down.'

'No, I'm definitely not out to tame Ben Dale. Someone else can take that task on. As lovely as he is, I know it's time to move on. I'd rather be alone than hanging onto him just for the sake of it.'

'I suppose you know what's best,' Scarlett said.

'The thing is,' Ava said, feeling the gin go to her head, 'I think I had the one, and let him get away. Isn't that the saddest love story you've ever heard?'

Chapter 24

'Hey, Ava, where have you been hiding?'

Ava nearly jumped out of her skin. 'Jesus, Finlay, you scared the bejaysus out of me. What are you doing creeping up on me?' She had just locked her car door and was about to go into Moonstone Street to pick up the post. Scarlett was staying there until she found something more permanent. An arrangement which suited them both.

'Sorry I didn't mean to frighten you. I was just waiting around hoping to see you.'

'What? Have you forgotten my phone number already?'

'You never seem to be in. Out with Ben a lot, it seems.' Finlay looked directly into her eyes, and Ava could have sworn he looked ever so slightly jealous.

'What if I have? Sure, you have the beautiful Rose to keep you entertained. Didn't take you long to move on.' Ava threw back at him with more spite in her tone than she intended.

'Look, can I come in?' He looked a bit sad, forlorn, his forehead creased in a frown.

'Sure, come on ahead.' Ava unlocked the door, bent down to pick up a couple of letters and led Finlay up the narrow hallway; both sides of which she could easily touch — if she stretched out her arms — from the age of eight.

'Christ, Ava, have you been away? Look at the amount of post,' said Finlay, full of concern as he picked up the embankment pile of junk mail and bills.

Ava laughed. 'No, I've moved out. This place looks a bit empty as I took some bits of furniture with me.' She looked around. It was the same as always only a bit dusty and neglected and was now missing the coffee table which she had poached the week before.

'Moved out? God, have you moved in with *him*?' Finlay asked, his voice cracking slightly.

'Who? With Ben? Catch yourself on. I have not indeed,' Ava said, suddenly pleased to think Finlay would be bothered if she had. Jealousy had never played a part in their relationship. They each had been so sure of the other to have made petty jealousies irrelevant.

'I have my own home now, off the Stranmillis Road over in Malone. I thought it was time to move out of here.' She looked wistfully around the half-empty room. Some things she had taken out of necessity and others were of sentimental value — the clock which had sat on the mantle throughout Ava's childhood, the little figurine of the shepherdess — all tat really, but they had always been there and she felt that they deserved a place in her new home. Scarlett had little to unpack and most of her things were in Maggie's old bedroom.

'Cup of tea?' Ava asked.

He nodded, his presence filling up the tiny kitchen.

She told him all about number ninety-seven, how she came to own it and her plans to do it up. They chatted away as easily as they had always done, comfortable in each other's company.

'And you had no idea your mum had bought this big house for you and Maggie to live in all those years ago?'

'No. Amanda my solicitor said she had instructions to have the house signed over to me by a third party. My gran had the sense to have it signed over in the event of her being incapacitated. When she had the stroke, I had to get power of attorney to manage her finances, and that triggered the house being signed over to me,' Ava said. 'But in clearing out some of Maggie's old papers and rubbish I came across a letter from her telling me all about the house, and then out of the blue, Scarlett arrives. She had been notified that the house had been transferred to me, so she assumed my gran had died. It's sad to think she thought her mother was dead but now finds her still alive. It's all sort of wonderful really.'

Ava could hardly believe they had spent the best part of an hour sitting in Moonstone Street's tiny kitchen, drinking tea. Scarlett was out exploring the city. She had told Ava the day before that she was trying to reacquaint herself with her old hometown.

Sitting here with Finlay, Ava felt as if they had never been apart, but yet something was different. She couldn't ignore the sparks of attraction she felt sitting in such close proximity to him. She kept noticing things about him that she had never taken the time to consider before, like the way he rubbed the back of his neck when he was thinking, the way his T-shirt stretched tight across his chest, showing his well-defined pec muscles, and the way his jeans creased around his groin. God, she had to get a grip of herself. What was she doing stealing glances of his nether regions?

'Still, it's all a bit strange,' he mused, oblivious to the effect he was having on her.

'Would you come around some evening and have a look at the electrics for me?'

'Of course, I will, any time.' He smiled, as if pleased to have been asked.

'You know I really like your new hair colour,' he said. 'It reminds me of conkers and autumn time.'

'Gee, thanks. I look like a conker,' deadpanned Ava.

'A very beautiful conker,' he replied, looking straight into her eyes.

'Oh, that's all right then.' She smiled at him, feeling the tight furls of protection unwind ever so slightly from her damaged heart.

Chapter 25

Ava didn't think anything of Hazel not showing up for work on Monday. Every now and then Hazel would give herself a day off, to go shopping for baby equipment, do her prenatal yoga class or have a relaxing spa treatment at her favourite beauty salon, Factor One in Carryduff.

Ava was well used to running the place alone. She did the stocktake, made the necessary orders, replenished the shelves when they were low on scented candles and deposited the takings in the Bank of Ireland. Trade was steady, but they had no weddings for the next two weeks so it was quiet enough.

But when Hazel still hadn't shown her face on Thursday, Ava began to worry. At closing time, she brought Hazel's mobile number up on her phone and hit the green dial button.

'Hello.' Strangely, it was Robert answering.

'Hiya, Robert. It's just Ava here. I was wondering if Hazel is all right. I haven't seen her for a few days and I wanted to check in with her.'

'Oh, Ava, yeah, sorry I should have called. She isn't feeling too good, bad case of the runs. I'll get her to call you when she picks up. Everything okay with the shop?'

'Yes, it's all fine. Tell her to take care and I'll see her when she's feeling better. Bye.'

Ava closed her phone and frowned. That was strange. Normally Hazel was one of those people who were surgically attached to their mobile, and if you wanted to make excuses and throw someone off the scent you told them it was a bad case of the runs. No one liked to admit to having the runs, especially not someone like Hazel who would rather die than make a reference to sitting on the loo.

Something was definitely up and she hoped that it had nothing to do with her and Ben.

God, if Hazel had found out, she would be horrified. She would brand Ava a dirty slag who had violated her precious, innocent son. Gone would be her memories of Ben, the chip off the old man's block, who had a series of girls traipsing in and out of Hazel's immaculate home. Ava was mortified at the thought of Hazel and Robert discussing how she had probably led their son astray.

She couldn't believe how bloody stupid she had been. There was one golden rule of friendship, never sleep with your best friend's boyfriend, ex or otherwise. But the golden rule should have had an appendage: definitely never sleep with your friend's son, even if he is old enough to make his own choices and cute enough to be hard to resist.

Still, no excuses. Ava had slipped up big time and she could have hurt Hazel when she was particularly vulnerable. Hazel probably couldn't bring herself to face Ava. She would probably leave a pay cheque on the counter at the end of the week for Ava to find with a note saying, *Leave the keys and don't come back, you slag*.

It was closing time on Friday when Robert turned up, his normally ruddy complexion looking ashen and his eyes searching the stock on the shelves, doing anything to avoid looking directly at Ava.

'Thought I'd drop by, see if you needed anything and check the takings,' he said, still not looking at Ava directly.

'How's Hazel?' Ava asked, her heart jumping in her chest, waiting for the moment Robert would hand her over wages and tell her not to come back.

But instead of rounding on her, he slumped like a broken man, his broad shoulders shaking ever so slightly.

'Oh, Ava, Hazel's in a right state,' he said, turning towards her for the first time and letting her see his tired and sad eyes.

'Look, Robert, all I can say is I'm sorry. Really truly sorry.' Ava took a deep breath and let the rest tumble out of her. 'I was drunk the first time when we were in your bed. I don't know why we ended up in your room rather than his. I can only assume his room was too messy. I like Ben, but I know I should never have allowed it to happen. It was only a couple of times, and we're just friends now. He understood that I couldn't risk hurting Hazel. Do you think she will ever forgive me?'

'What? You and our *Ben*?' he asked, his eyes widening in surprise. 'No offence, Ava, but I didn't see that one coming.' He even smiled, his mournful eyes lighting up for a few seconds.

'Oh, God, isn't that what this is all about? Hazel avoiding me, you coming in to let me go?'

Robert's eyes crinkled up and in spite of himself, let out a roar of laughter. Ava knew Robert's laugh; it was full and robust, a bit like himself.

'Oh, God, I needed that,' he said, wiping his eyes with the back of his hand. 'I haven't cracked a smile in days.'

'If you didn't know about me and Ben, then what's going on?' Ava said, a mixture of relief and then fresh worry washing over her.

'Come on, Ava, let's go for a drink. I think we both need one.'

They parked their bums on the wooden church pews in the Empire bar, each clutching their drink as a buttress to what was to come.

'So, what's going on? Is it the baby? God, she hasn't had a miscarriage, has she?' Ava asked, her eyes full of concern.

'Yes, it's the baby, but no we haven't lost it.' He took a gulp of his pint of Guinness then licked the creamy white foam off his top lip. 'No, the doctors have put her on bedrest. She was bleeding a bit and having pains, so it's just to be sure.'

'Oh, Robert, I'm sorry. God, poor Hazel, she must be worried sick. No wonder she hasn't been in work.'

He nodded. 'I know she has spent the whole of her pregnancy worrying about things that could go wrong, but I never really believed that anything bad would happen. She sailed through the boys' pregnancies. There was none of this testing for everything back in those days so you were just delighted when they were born and you could count the ten fingers and toes. We never really knew much about what could go wrong then. But nowadays, they have tests for everything, and with Hazel getting on, they were treating her like it was to be expected.'

Ava put her hand on his arm and squeezed it to let him know how deeply sorry she was. The pregnancy may have been an unexpected surprise, but Ava knew how loved and wanted the baby was. It wasn't fair that they should have to deal with something so sad.

'So, you can imagine we have been lying low, trying to get our heads around being older parents.' He supped his pint then stroked the cool wet glass as if caressing a dutiful pet.

'I understand. It would take a while to let it sink in and to accept.'

'Yeah, at the beginning, Hazel did a bit of crying, but you know what, she never once thought not to have it. She just said we were lucky to be having a wee surprise baby come our way. You just have to crack on with it.' He smiled. 'Made me love her all the more. So, the thought of losing the baby now...' he trailed off.

'She's a good mother and you're a good husband and father, Robert. It'll work out,' said Ava, filled with admiration for the poor man who was obviously trying to hold his emotions in check and to give Hazel the support she needed.

'I suppose so. What else can we do? Life just throws things at you and you either run with the ball or drop it.'

They drank up and said their goodbyes both of them feeling emotionally rung out.

'Tell Hazel that the shop is ticking over and not to worry; I have it all under control. I'm here if she needs me to talk or just be a shoulder to cry on but I understand if she needs some space at the minute,' Ava said, giving Robert a hug.

'You're a great girl, Ava. Our Ben would have been a lucky lad to get a girl like you to stick around. Do me a favour though — don't go confessing anything to our Hazel. She's feeling so emotional at the minute that I wouldn't want to try second-guess how she would react. She loves you, don't get me wrong, but where Ben's concerned nobody is too good or even good enough. I know I could take the ear bashing for not letting on to her that you've told me, but she is like a bag of cats at the minute, and I don't want her going off in the deep end again.' He waved goodbye and headed off home.

Ava watched him wander off up Botanic Avenue, his head down and shoulders hunched up around his ears as if had to take on the world.

Chapter 26

Ava watched the bubbles rise upwards in her champagne flute. She lifted the glass to her lips and took a sip. The chocolate-covered strawberries were the perfect compliment, and while the thought of an afternoon of high tea indulgence at the Merchant hotel should have filled her with a sense of contentment, she wasn't exactly stoked about the whole set-up.

The big three-oh had finally arrived. Niamh had insisted in a girly tea party and had invited Hazel and Scarlett along. They all seemed to be getting on just fine, but Ava's mind kept drifting. Thinking of Finlay and other birthdays she had spent with him. She couldn't help feeling disappointed that he hadn't called or sent a card.

She had woken early and popped over to Moonstone Street just to check if he had posted a card there. But no, nothing. The disappointment that he hadn't bothered to remember her on her birthday had put the dampeners on the whole day. Joseph had text and sent a selfie, pointing to a restaurant called Squid Ink.

Joseph: *Happy birthday, Squid girl! This restaurant awaits your order, should you ever take me up on the offer of a holiday.*

If it weren't for worrying about Maggie, Ava would have happily booked a flight. That would have been one sure way of getting over Finn.

'There's a girl on a shoot we were doing last week who had her hen week in Ibiza. She was telling me how they all went to this brilliant foam party and got off with these gorgeous fellas from Swansea,' Niamh was saying.

'What about the bride? Did she pull a fella as well?' asked Hazel, biting into her white chocolate-covered strawberry.

'She had a wee bit of a snog but nothing full on. She was getting married after all.' Niamh laughed as she helped herself to another glass of champagne.

'I don't think Robert would have approved of me having a bit of a snog, even on my hen night,' laughed Hazel.

They pored over the tea menu as they sat taking in the sumptuous surroundings of the former bank's Great Room Restaurant. They ordered the three-tiered silver stand of finger sandwiches, scones with clotted cream and jam and a selection of cakes, pastries and sweet treats.

'In LA, they hold pre-wedding showers like this only you can have Botox, chemical facial peels and collagen fillers while you eat,' said Scarlett.

'I read that there is a plastic surgeon in America who performs "female enhancement surgery" for women wishing to be virginal tight on their wedding night,' said Niamh.

Ava pulled a face. 'Ew. The very thought of it is enough to put me off my strawberries.'

Chapter 27

Later that evening, Ava and Scarlett went to visit Maggie. She was becoming more alert again and seemed to have improved. Every now and then she would lapse into talking about the old days, as if they were children sitting at Maggie's knee. Scarlett's presence seemed to please and confuse her all at once.

'Hiya, Gran. How are you feeling today?' asked Ava.

'The clock is ticking. I can hear it, yet my hearing isn't good. It's strange when I know it's standing like a sentinel out in the hallway out of sight. I see it when they wheel me out to the bathroom; it stands watching me, marking time. Funny to hear it now. It doesn't chime, just ticks. Things come and go: memories, senses, voices. I've learnt not to fear them when they come or miss them when they are gone.'

'It's going to be one of those nights,' Ava whispered to Scarlett.

'Is that you, Ava? Sit a while. Stop fussing with my pillows and let me look at you. Your eyes are glistening. Your cheeks are all a glow. Like a little girl come in out of the cold, smelling of gingerbread and oranges.

'Do you remember Halloween? Carving out turnips making them into lanterns, the smell of the candle flame scorching the inside of it, and the horrible smell reeking through the house. Oh, but you loved it. Scarlett sent you over that wee witch's costume with the broom and the hat. Nobody over here had ever seen the likes of it. Of course, nowadays they all have their fancy dress outfits, but in those days, it was a real novelty. Your wee face was a picture when you looked in the mirror to see yourself all dressed up.'

'I remember that outfit, Mum. I bought it in a shop on Santa Monica strip,' Scarlett said, smiling. 'I missed so much, Mum, didn't I?' She sat next to Maggie, while Ava busied herself tidying the room.

Maggie pursed her lips together, too wise to admonish Scarlett, since she was back, Ava thought. Neither of them wanted to risk her running off again, now that they had her in their lives. Ava could hardly believe it.

Maggie reached out and took Scarlett's hand. 'I can see the past so clearly, snatches of conversation run through my head like a radio play. Sometimes I can even taste things from long ago: Bird's custard, brown lemonade, cough drops, clove rock. Silly really, how my mind can trick me.

'For a second, I forget age has shackled me and I believe that I can throw my legs over the bed with the abandon of youth and run out the door. But then I feel the numbness, the aches or the sharp flinches of pain reminding me of my age like a suit of armour clinking to sound out my limitations. Not that I mind really. When you get to my age... what am I... eighty-six? I'm never sure these days. You are ready to give up all that which you thought was so important: the house kept tidy and clean, the new coat hanging in the wardrobe, the trinkets we gather over the years as if they mean something.'

Scarlett took Maggie's hand. 'Mum, I'm so glad to be here with you.'

Chapter 28

Ava was serving a regular customer when the telephone rang. Hazel took the call and when Ava had rung the order into the till and said cheerio, Hazel handed the phone to Ava. 'It's Niamh. She sounds a bit upset.'

Ava took the phone out to the back kitchen, suddenly worried. 'Hi, Niamh?'

'Ava – it's my dad, he died last night.' She sniffed, obviously making an effort to remain calm and collected.

'Oh, honey. Where are you?'

'Up at my mum's. The undertakers are here.' She hiccupped, her voice breaking up with emotion.

'Listen, sit tight. I'll let Hazel know and try to get straight up to you.'

'Thanks, Ava.'

'No problem. I'll see you in a bit.' She hit the red end button and went out to the shop front to tell Hazel what had happened. 'I'm going to have to head up to her house, can you manage without me?'

'Sure, don't worry. I'll phone Erin and see if she can come in for a few hours. She can normally drop her wee boy off at her mum's at short notice,' Hazel said, her face full of concern for Niamh.

The night before had been freezing cold and the gritters had been out trying to make the roads safe. Ava drove slowly up the icy Shore Road dreading reaching Mrs Lenaghan's house. Niamh's family were tight knit. She had three older brothers, all successful in their chosen careers and married with young families of their own.

Throughout her friendship with Niamh, Ava had come to know and love the Lenaghan family as if it were an extension of her own. While she was used to the quiet, contemplative atmosphere of living with Maggie in Moonstone Street, she relished her times amongst the noisy, vibrant Lenaghan. They thought nothing of fighting and cursing in front of Ava, so used were they to her company it was as if she was one of their own. But despite this familiarity, and while she may have stayed at their house many times during her teenage years and gone to stay in their holiday cottage in Donegal on a few occasions, she always called them Mr and Mrs Lenaghan. Mr Lenaghan had even taken pity on Ava's sorry attempts to learn to drive when he had discovered the instructor had more lecherous intentions in mind than watching the road ahead. The instructor's fumbling attempts to seduce her in his Ford Fiesta while extolling Ava to keep looking ahead and read the road backfired when she rammed the car into the back of a bus.

Mr Lenaghan, incensed when he heard about the driving instructor, had taken it upon himself to teach Ava how to drive and couldn't have been prouder when she passed first time.

Ava had often been a little jealous of the easy, boisterous fashion the Lenaghans lived in. Their house wasn't small but it always felt as if it were bursting at the seams, so packed was it with cousins and all sorts of friends of Niamh's brothers. Mrs Lenaghan was a seamstress by trade who worked from home when her family came along. She had turned her front room into a sewing room and Niamh and Ava loved going in to look at the bridesmaid dresses as they progressed from the cutting table to the tailor's dummy standing in the front bay window and the dozens of shades of threads and fabrics she kept there. Mrs Lenaghan could rustle up a rah-rah skirt or shorten an old pair of trousers into a pair of pedal pushers in half an hour, and many a time Ava and Niamh were kitted out in clothes to make the rest of their classmates envious.

Ava hit her indicator on before swerving into the Lenaghans' road. She skidded slightly on part of the icy road the gritters had failed to cover. The freezing cold spell in Northern Ireland was a bit like the rain, predictable but, as usual, it had taken everyone by surprise.

The Lenaghans had moved to North Belfast when Niamh was twelve which resulted in her having to ride two buses every day to be at the same grammar school as Ava. But everyone travelled to school, catchment areas being a thing associated with across the water. In Belfast, if you had to travel to attend the religious school of your persuasion then so be it.

Their semi-detached house was situated at the bottom of Cave Hill, which dominated the skyline of North Belfast. Ava and Niamh had been forced to climb the hills on a couple of occasions by Mr Lenaghan in his determination to educate the girls about their city. He would tell them stories of how the basaltic hill, formed millions of years earlier, had been originally named Ben Madigan, and how the rock formation which appeared to look like the profile of Napoleon from afar had served as the inspiration for the novel Gulliver's Travels.

The country park of the surrounding area had become known as Cave Hill from the five caves which were thought to be early iron mines found on the side of the cliffs. Most of the time, Ava and Niamh had huffed and puffed their way up the grassy rock, resentful of having to spend their Saturday morning away from Rugrats, but when they reached the plateau, tired and breathless, and saw the breath-taking view over the city and the Lough their grumpiness dissipated and they fell under the spell of the Cave Hill walk. It had been years since they had done that walk but Ava still remember with crystal clarity the look of satisfaction on Mr Lenaghan's face when Niamh's whining had been silenced by the magnificent view.

Ava had to park opposite the Lenaghans' house. A black hearse was parked in their narrow driveway and many cars cluttered the normally empty road. A couple of men she didn't recognised stood solemnly outside the house smoking and talking in hushed voices.

She noticed the streetlights were glowing orange despite it being mid-morning, as if to signify that everything in the world was upside down and wrong.

Ava nodded to them and walked through the wide-open door. She could hear Niamh speaking to her mother. 'Mummy, come on now. You need to get dressed.' She seemed to be trying to coax the catatonic woman to go up the stairs and put a more suitable outfit on than the haphazard one she was wearing and had obviously pulled together in haste when Mr Lenaghan had taken ill the previous night.

Ava made her way on into the long galley kitchen and put the kettle on. She lifted a couple of mugs off the draining board, gave them a rinse and set about making coffee. Ava was familiar with the lay out of the pristine kitchen and knew where to find sugar and biscuits. What was it about catastrophe and death to make people reach for the kettle? *I suppose it's something to do*, she thought, as she filled two mugs with boiling water. She stared out of the kitchen window across the frost-covered lawn to the shed where Mr Lenaghan had done his potting.

A few minutes later, Niamh came into the kitchen.

'Thanks for coming,' she said, her face mottled red and puffy with crying.

'Come here.' Ava hugged Niamh and felt her shoulders tense and shudder as if she were making a Herculean effort to hold herself together.

'Oh, Ava, it was awful. Mummy phoned me and I met her over at the Royal but it was too late they couldn't do anything; he was already gone in the ambulance. It was his heart. The ambulance man explained that they had worked on him for a good hour, laid out on the hall floor, trying to bring him back, but it was no good.' Her chest heaved.

Niamh looked so young with her face bare of make-up and her pinky-blonde hair sticking up at odd angles. She was wearing a blue striped pyjama top over a pair of jeans and had an old pair of trainers on her feet with no socks. Ava wrapped her arms around Niamh and let her pour her heart out. She sobbed and rocked, and mumbled about not being there when he died, and how was she ever going to ask him to forgive her for all the things she had done wrong in her life.

Ava shushed her and stroked her soft hair, knowing that there was nothing she could say to offer solace. The pain and the heartache would need time to subside.

The house became a hive of people over the next few days. People came day and night to pay their respects and view the corpse. Mr Lenaghan had many friends and ensuring a good wake was their way of honouring his memory.

On the second night, Ava insisted Mrs Lenaghan and Niamh went to bed to get some rest before the funeral the following day. They were both worn out, tired from the strain of entertaining well-intentioned callers, making endless cups of tea and sandwiches and doing anything but sit still and talk about the man who had left a massive hole in their lives. It was as if they were hiding from their grief, trying to out run its heavy cast iron grip which would floor them the second they acknowledged it.

'But I need to speak to the priest and make sure everything is in order for tomorrow,' protested Mrs Lenaghan as Ava tried to cajole her into going up to bed.

'Now come on, leave the poor priest alone. You have near enough told him how to bless himself with the orders you have been giving out to him all day. Everything is sorted. The boys are downstairs and will deal with any stragglers coming to say their last goodbyes. I want you and Niamh to have some sleep. You both will need your strength for tomorrow.'

The weary woman bowed her head and let Ava steer her towards her bedroom. The bed was perfectly made up, with no sign of the panic and disarray of the night her husband had felt the first crushing band of pain in his chest.

'You know when it happened he looked at me and said, "This is it, Mary. I'm on my way out" and do you know I says to him, catch yer self on I'm too busy this week to be organising a funeral. I didn't mean it, but now I haven't got him to make fun of.' She shuddered, her body convulsing in sobs.

Ava held her tight and let the crying pass in its own time. 'He knew you loved him. We all did.'

'You're a good girl, Ava. Eamonn always said you were a good influence on our Niamh.' Mrs Lenaghan gave Ava a quick, tight hug and settled herself on top of the bedclothes. 'I'll not get undressed, I'll just lie here a wee while and rest my eyes and if anyone needs me you'll come right up and get me.'

'Of course. Now pull that comforter over you and let me take care of things downstairs.'

Ava knew Mrs Lenaghan would be asleep in minutes. The poor woman had been without sleep for two nights, and was still reeling from the shock.

Ava knocked gently on Niamh's bedroom door, before peeking in. In the pale grey light she could see the outline of Niamh huddled under the duvet and hear her snuffling loudly.

'It's only me. Can I get you anything?' Ava asked.

'No,' she mumbled and sniffed again. Ava walked over and sat on the bed beside her. The room hadn't changed much from the days when Niamh lived there and they both had spent nights reading Mallory Towers novels to later moving onto contraband Jackie Collins and whispering to each other for fear of waking Niamh's parents. The walls were painted a pale sickly pink and the floor was still covered with the same blue and pink swirled-patterned carpet.

Ava could remember sleeping head to toe with Niamh and waking up to find a toe practically lodged in her ear.

'Do you remember the time he drove me to Dublin to start my make-up artistry course? He really didn't want me to move away and he thought training to do make-up for people was the greatest waste of time and money. He said his bit, but once he knew I wasn't going to be swayed easily, he helped me pack up my stuff and drove me there.

'The whole way down to Dublin, we laughed and joked, and I felt like I was seven again and he was my whole world. By the time I got to Dublin, I felt homesick and didn't know if I could go through with it, and he just gave me a hug and said he'd be back for me in a fortnight and if I didn't want to stay, he'd take me home then, but I would have to give it a go or I'd be blaming him for ruining my chances of doing make-up for some big Hollywood star.

'Of course, he knew fine well I'd love it and it was his way of letting me go. He said he never wanted to let me go without a fight.'

'You were lucky to have him.' Ava stroked Niamh's arm.

'I know but it just makes it all the harder losing him. I never made much effort for him of late. Sure, I came over for my dinner on Sundays and if I was stuck for money I would drop by his office, but I didn't go for walks with him anymore or listen to his stories. Why didn't I see he wouldn't be here forever?'

'Try to get some sleep. You will collapse tomorrow if you don't. I'll go down and see the boys and head on home. I'll be here first thing in the morning.'

'Okay, thanks, Ava.'

Niamh's brothers were gathered in the kitchen with their two uncles, who had travelled from England for their brother's wake and funeral. They were drinking beers and eating the endless sandwiches and cakes, brought by neighbours and friends. Their voices rose and fell away like the ebb of the sea. She decided not to disturb them and thought she should take a moment to say her own private goodbye to Mr Lenaghan.

Ava paused before going into the front room. Mrs Lenaghan's sewing paraphernalia had been moved to make space for the coffin. A tall vase containing calla lilies, sent by Hazel, stood in the hearth with two blessed candles, thick and creamy white, on either side held erect in two elaborate silver candle sticks. Their flames had been extinguished but the smell of melted wax still hung in the room along with the perfume of the flowers.

In all of the arrangements and the coming and going between checking in on Maggie and looking after Niamh, Ava had yet to view the corpse. When the body had been returned from hospital, with the news they all knew — he had suffered a massive coronary — Ava had hung back and allowed the family time with their father alone. She hadn't wanted to intrude.

As the following day passed with a constant stream of visitors paying their respects, she was busy making teas and coffees and washing up to do it all again.

This had been her first opportunity to say goodbye. She crossed the room, edged with chairs for the many visitors to sit on, and looked down on Mr Lenaghan. His skin looked waxen and stretched, while his pallor was as milky white as porridge. Out of respect, she crossed herself and mumbled a prayer.

Chapter 29

'Evie is a lovely name,' said Ava.

Hazel smiled looking into the Perspex crib beside her bed. 'We're calling her Evangeline but it is such a big name for a little girl so we'll shorten it to Evie. She suits it, doesn't she?'

'Yeah, she really does,' said Ava as she stared down at Evie, content in a deep sleep, her little chest rising and falling softly with every breath.

'Do you want to hold her?' Hazel asked.

'Oh, I don't want to wake her,' Ava replied, terrified of lifting the rosy pink-skinned infant. Finlay would have scooped her up in an instant but Ava was less familiar with newborns. As if on cue, the sleeping Evie stretched out her little arms and opened her eyes. She blinked at the bright hospital lights and opened and closed her mouth as if trying it out before crying.

'There you go; she wants you to lift her up. She won't break but watch she is a bit floppy,' Hazel said.

Ava's heart contracted and missed a beat as she carefully lifted the little baby into her arms and cradled her close to her chest. Evie's pale rose pink lips were pressed tight together as if to say you can cuddle me but don't disturb me, her nose a little button of cuteness and her fine blonde hair like wisps of candy floss.

'Oh, she is so gorgeous,' Ava said in a whisper, her heart filled with awe at the tiny scrap of life in her arms.

'I know,' Hazel murmured, her face lit up with love. 'We can hardly believe how beautiful she is. I can't stop staring at her. Even when I know I should be trying to sleep, I just lie there looking at her in amazement.'

Hazel was sitting up in the hospital bed wearing her dove grey lace and silk nightdress, her skin glowing with a little help from her tinted moisturiser, concealer wand and highlighter cream. She had taken care to pile her hair up into a sexy French roll, looking as glamorous and groomed as usual, despite having spent eighteen hours in labour the previous day. Ava knew Hazel wasn't going to have people saying she had let herself go just because she had a new baby to look after.

'The nurses cluck around her like she is an angel sent from heaven. Everyone has been so kind and caring,' Hazel said as she reached her hand over to touch the soft velvet skin of her newborn daughter's face.

'Robert bawled his eyes out when she was born. He held my hand so tightly I thought he had crushed a few bones! But he was very brave, even went down below for a look when her head was crowning and him so squeamish and all. I thought he would have passed out or run away, but he was great,' Hazel said, overflowing with pride. 'He can hardly believe he has a daughter. Keeps calling her his wee princess. And the boys have been lovely; nursing her and bringing her little gifts.'

'How are you feeling?' Ava asked, her eyes full of concern for her friend.

'I'm grand. Bit wobbly on my feet for the first six hours but that was just the epidural still in my system. I've no stitches, and all being well with Evie, we will be home tomorrow.'

'No blubbering yet?'

'No, but one of the night nurses sat with me last night and warned me that when the milk hormones kick in I might feel a bit down and weepy. Listen, it goes with the territory. I know what to expect.'

'When did you get to be so wise and philosophical?' Ava asked, handing the now-mewling infant back to her mother with care.

'Oh, I don't know. Maybe having her so late in life has been a good thing. But don't go holding me to all this wise woman wisdom. It's probably the hormones speaking but you know what,

I just want to enjoy her.' Hazel put baby Evie to her chest and using her free hand scooped out a breast and directed it to the child's mouth, trying to encourage her to latch on.

'At the minute, the hardest thing has been helping her eat. The nurses keep forcing formula on me telling me she'll not manage to suck but I want to keep trying to feed her myself.'

'I hear Robert has been busy painting the nursery,' Ava said.

'Yeah. Even though we knew she was a girl after the amino test came back, we couldn't bring ourselves to start the decorating until she was here, just in case. I didn't want to tempt fate. But sure, look at her, she's just perfect,' Hazel sighed.

She was. Ava could see she was really just perfect.

Chapter 30

Ava was clearing up for the night. The shop had been busy all day, and although she had help from the part-time girl, Erin, Ava was exhausted. She just had the rubbish to put out for the bin men and then she could go home. A hot bath followed by a plate of scrambled eggs and toast with a nice cup of strong tea in front of Netflix beckoned.

Hazel was still on maternity leave but Ava was beginning to doubt if she would ever be able to drag herself away from Evie. The shop was so far down on Hazel's list of priorities that if it burnt to the ground, Ava doubted Hazel would care. Still, when she did eventually emerge from her maternal stupor, Ava wanted to ensure that Hazel had a well-run business to return to.

Ava opened the back door of the little yard to set the rubbish bags out when she thought she saw something move. It was hard to see since the yard was so overlooked by the neighbouring shops that it was always cast in shadow at that time of night. She didn't feel like waiting around so she hurried back into the shop with her heart thumping. *God, catch yerself on*, she admonished. It was probably only some old stray cat or at worse a rat.

Ava grabbed her bag and her coat, set the alarm, and headed out to her car. She was just pulling the front shutter down when she heard a voice call out, 'Hey you.'

She turned and saw someone come out from the entryway which ran down behind the row of shops. Ava near enough jumped out of her skin.

'If you think you are going to get away with this you can think again.'

'Sorry, do I know you?' Ava asked trying to sound dismissive and confident when she was actually quaking in her fake Ugg boots.

'You certainly know my boyfriend,' the girl snarled. She had hair the colour of cherries and it was cut into a harsh bob, all razor edged and precise.

'I think you're mixing me up with someone else,' said Ava, trying to turn the lock in the key even though her hand was shaking. This girl was young and slightly built but she seemed unreasonably aggressive and wasn't making any sense.

'Ben Dale? I'm sure that rings a bell.' She practically spat the words out as if they were a challenge.

'Who are you?' Ava asked, pretty sure she knew the answer already.

'Mickey, his *girlfriend*, and if you want to keep your little flower arranging job you can back off and leave my man alone.' She turned on her spiked-heeled boots and strode away up Botanic Avenue, leaving Ava with a thumping heartbeat and a dry mouth.

'What? Mickey? And she threatened you, like?' Ben said scratching his stubble, his eyes wide.

'Not in so many words but she certainly made her point. Said I had to back off or I'd lose my job. Shit, Ben, what if she tells your mum?' Ava was still shaken up. She knew enough from Hazel to know that Mickey could be a bit off the wall and crazily possessive of Ben.

'But I haven't been going out with Mickey for over a month now.'

'You could try making sure she knows that,' Ava said. 'I don't appreciate people creeping up on me like that and being nasty.'

'Hey, babe. I'm sorry if she upset you. God, I'll have a word with her. Trouble is I bet if I ring her, it will be near enough an open invitation in her mind to get back together. She had me tortured for months. It was like going out with a sticking plaster;

she couldn't bear not to be holding hands or kissing, and then if I tried to have any time with me mates she became all moody and jealous. She did my head in.'

'Yeah, your mum told me about her. But just make sure Mickey knows we aren't an item.'

'Sure, I'll try.'

Chapter 31

When the call came, Ava had been dragging the old carpet from the stairs in Mount Pleasant Square. She stopped and threw down the heavy carpet, sweat and dirt clinging to her, and took out her phone. It was the Sisters of Mercy care home. They never phoned without good reason. Ava's heart raced as she answered. 'Hello?'

'Ava, it's Sister Lucy here. I'm afraid Maggie has had a turn. We've called the doctor and he's on his way.'

'I'll be right there.' Ava hung up and locked up the house, not caring that she was covered in dust and wearing her paint-splattered joggers.

The drive to the care home seemed to take an eternity but when she arrived Sister Lucy ushered her in.

'She's okay. The doctor says it's another stroke. He's still with her, checking her obs.'

Ava made her way down to Maggie's room where she found the doctor packing up to go.

'How is she?' Ava asked.

'All okay for now. I don't see the point in moving her to the hospital. I phoned through to the ward and spoke to the consultant, and she is happy enough to let her rest.'

'Okay, thank you.'

A week later, Ava gently brushed Maggie's almost snow-white hair. She had rallied round and was slowly regaining her awareness of where she was and who was with her. It had been a sharp reminder of how time was evaporating. Each day was a day closer to when she wouldn't be there.

Ava could see with a new clarity how much of Maggie's life had been dedicated to her family. Loving and caring for her husband, seeing him off to work at the Water Board with his freshly packed Tupperware lunchbox, and his smartly pressed and starched overalls, and then later, looking after the wayward Scarlett, only to lose her to the bright lights of stardom and to find consolation in caring for her daughter Ava. Maggie represented a dying breed of women who literally lived for their family. She sought nothing beyond the four walls of her little neat and sparkling clean terrace house, happy to spend her days with a bottle of Mr Sheen in one hand and a yellow duster in the other.

Scarlett's desire to seek a life elsewhere was the antithesis of Maggie's dreams. How it must have puzzled and confused the woman to see such yearnings in her daughter, Ava thought.

Ava could see how the mother and daughter would have clashed, neither appreciating nor caring for the other's way of life, their differences exacerbated by the blood bonds connecting them.

The nurse came in to check the monitor and to take Maggie's blood pressure.

'How is it?' asked Ava.

'A bit low but nothing we wouldn't expect. She's made of stern stuff so don't be worrying. Doctor Napier expects she will pick up over the next couple of days. He just wants to keep a close eye on her and make sure she isn't about to have another stroke.'

The nurse entered the information on the chart hanging at the bottom of the bed, squirted a dollop of antibacterial gel on her hands before she wheeled her blood pressure machine back out of the room.

'There, did you hear that, Gran? The doctor expects you to feel better over the next couple of days. You just have to keep fighting. Don't go giving up on me just yet, do you hear?' Ava bit back the tears. She didn't want to upset Maggie by crying and although she seemed to be out of it, she could perhaps sense that all wasn't well with Ava. From when Ava was knee high, Maggie could read her moods and knew when to scoop her up for a big warm, floury smelling hug. Maggie hadn't been one for sloppy kisses or cuddles but when needed she could dole out the best hugs and make everything better just by being there.

Ava couldn't imagine how she would feel if Maggie didn't make it back this time. Each stroke seemed to carry her further away, deeper into ineptitude and dependency. Their conversations were drying up. It was as if they hardly knew how to be with each other without illness and age between them.

Ava sat watching Maggie, happy to be in her company, but remembering other days when they could talk with ease about nothing of importance.

How they had squandered that carefree time.

Chapter 32

'I don't get it,' Finlay said as he stared out across the river, its slick, grey surface bubbling and moving with intensity. They had gone for a walk, a ramble really, across muddy fields and through flooded lanes. The rain had been relentless over the previous week but had let up at last, making Ava feel that she had to get out into the fresh air while she could. She wanted to talk to Finlay about how she felt, and to do so indoors would feel too incendiary. Space and openness would allow the words to flow without bouncing back to her making her feel uncomfortable and self-conscious. She knew she had changed, but not that much. She still struggled to deal with how she felt and she wanted to try to make Finlay understand.

'I know I'm not making much sense but I feel as if I've just woken up. It's as if for the past God knows how many years, I've been in a fog of not feeling anything too deeply. I'm not saying I didn't love you, even then, when we were together, but it was just that I never let myself really *experience* it.'

'So, what's changed?' He turned to look at Ava, making her feel uncomfortable under his steady gaze.

'I've changed,' she said simply. 'Finding Scarlett, understanding why and even how she left me, has altered me. I know I probably sound as flaky as she is, but it's as if in finding her I've found myself.' How could she explain that her world had tilted like the sinking Titanic, and only with him could it rectify itself? She needed him to find her footing and although she knew that she would have to tread carefully, she wasn't about to walk away.

She hesitated, trying to find the right words to express the turmoil she had experienced which had given rise to this blissful sense of ease, of being *herself*. She was no longer acting out the role of being the good girl, frightened of living for fear of making mistakes in life. It was as if her whole life had been spent making up for Scarlett. Maggie had been her linchpin and her shackle. Without meaning to, she had created a sense of guilt and responsibility in Ava which she didn't deserve to carry. The sins of her mother had been visited upon her downy head from the moment Maggie had agreed to take her in. While she knew Maggie would never have intended to make Ava carry this burden, she also knew that she could at last shake it off. Scarlett's reappearance in her life had redressed a balance she had been lacking. It was as if in learning about her mother, her choices and her reasons, she was becoming more like the Ruby that Scarlett intended her to be and less like the Ava Maggie had invented.

He loved her once, *right?* So, he could love her again, only this time she would love him back, harder and faster than ever before.

His face was darkened with a shadow of unshaved stubble, his eyes stony and cold. She realised he was angry and she knew she couldn't blame him. He had processed the end of their relationship and had tied up all the pieces in his head before moving past all of this.

Ava was creating problems he didn't want or need to revisit or to resolve. At that moment, she feared she had lost him completely. He was already gone from her, never to return and the sadness of it felt like a cold stone of hurt buried within her very being.

'I know we have both moved on, but I just want you to understand. If you know how I feel then you can make your choice, but don't write me off because of how it was before.' She stopped her heart thumping to the rhythm of *It's over. You have no chance.*

At least it was out there, the words hanging on the breeze. She had said her bit. It was up to him now. She looked out towards the river tumbling, flowing fast with the new swell of the previous week's rainfall having inflated its width. The riverbanks were strained under the pressure to contain the water's urgency. If he wanted her, she was there for the taking. Maybe their relationship had run its course, and final and complete separation was long overdue, but she felt that there was so much more for them to explore in each other.

And then she was angry. Angry with him for letting her go so easily. If he had loved her truly then surely, he would have made it work? He would have fought to keep her instead of letting her blow away like a dandelion seed.

She turned away from the river and looked directly at Finlay. Something about him, the way he looked at her made her want to hit him hard. Was he laughing at her? She couldn't help it, she reached out and pushed him, wanting to make him angry, make him fight her and for their future together. He barely stumbled back, like her shove was so ineffectually to his brawny bulk, his white trainers making a squishy sound in the mud.

'What was that for?' he asked, righting his footing.

'Just coz you never tried to make me love you. You were happy to just let me walk away.' She knew she sounded unreasonable but she couldn't help it. Suddenly she felt like he had to care enough to make her love him back. Then, without warning, the ground shifted, a mudslide beneath Finlay's feet caused him to lose his balance and fall backwards down the riverbank. He grasped at the sodden grassy bank and Ava watched helplessly as he slid as if in slow motion into the river.

He stood up, dirty water dripping from his North Face jacket, his white shirt a dull sludgy brown and his face thunderous.

Ava couldn't help it. She laughed so hard she was bent double and took a cautionary step backwards in case the ground beneath her feet followed into the river too.

'I'm sorry to laugh,' she squeaked between gulps of laughter, 'but that is the funniest thing I've ever seen.' Tears careered down her face and she clutched at her sides.

She reached out to help him out of the cold, dank water.

He squelched his way up the riverbank, careful not to slide backwards.

I've blown it, she thought. He looked down at his jeans, soaking wet and brown with mud, his trainers destroyed and the bottom of his jacket dripping.

Before her thoughts could frighten her into taking back everything she had said, Finlay turned to her and taking her face in his hands, his cold, wet, dirty hands, he placed his soft, oh-so-soft, lips on hers, silencing the doubts and questions rushing through her head.

She broke away, wanting to look directly into his familiar eyes to see if he meant the kiss. She needed to know — was this for real and for good?

Chapter 33

Ava and Niamh were catching up over lunch. It had been a couple of weeks since the funeral and Ava was determined to make sure Niamh was doing okay. The waiter approached with his notepad poised to take their order.

'Mmm, I'll have the beetroot-cured salmon, horseradish and chive crème fraiche with a side order of wedges please,' said Niamh closing the menu and giving the attractive waiter one of her most dazzling smiles. In spite of being heartbroken with grief, she was still open to offers.

'And can I have the penne pasta, roasted butternut squash and tomatoes. Thanks.'

'No problem and can I get you two beautiful girls anything to drink?' he asked, returning the come-hither look Niamh was throwing him.

'I'll have a Coke please,' said Ava.

'And a sparkling water for me, thanks,' Niamh said casting her eyes down to look demure and bashful.

When he had gone, Ava rolled her eyes. 'You don't believe in taking breaks between lovers, do you?'

'Honey, life is too short. Besides it's a physical need with me. I'm not like you.'

'What's that supposed to mean?' asked Ava, feeling stung.

'Just that you're happy with yourself for company in bed. I, on the other hand, need a bit of a flesh fest going on between the sheets. I need a man to do the things a vibrator can't.'

'You don't know everything about me, Niamh Lenaghan,' Ava said, trying to look as if she was the keeper of secrets that Niamh knew nothing about.

'Such as? You can't hold out on me when I've told you all about my goings on.'

'For your information, Finlay and I might just be getting back together,' Ava said with a smug grin.

'Whoa, when did this happen?' Niamh asked wide-eyed with surprise.

'A couple of weeks ago. We talked, we held hands, we kissed. I'm hoping we can start over, take things slowly, and see how it goes.'

'So, what happened to his whole breaking-up speech about you not wanting him enough, and not being fully committed to him?'

'He can see things have changed. I don't want to hold back any more. I want him and I'll do whatever it takes to keep him,' Ava said in a matter-of-fact tone.

Niamh gasped in mock horror. 'I don't believe it. Ava Connors is talking like a real hot-blooded woman.'

'Better get used to it, coz I feel like I've a lot of catching up to do.' Ava snapped a bread stick in two.

'You need to stop talking about taking things slowly. If you want Finn back for good, you're going to have to prove it to him. Talk is all well and dandy, Ava, but you're going to have to prove to him you want him.'

Ava rolled her eyes. 'Niamh, don't be so melodramatic. Finn and I just need to reacquaint ourselves with each other and go on a few tentative dates.'

'Ava, have you learnt nothing from me and Cal? Have you forgotten about Rose, and how Finlay has been shagging her for the past few months?'

Ava blanched at the thought of Finlay with Rose. Did Niamh have to be so graphic? 'Maybe you're right.'

'Honey, you know I am. Think about it – Finlay was with you for eight years. Now, no offence, but you have to agree you were no wild, hot thing in the bedroom department, so you can be sure that when he made comparisons Rose will have scored considerably higher than you my friend.'

Ava suddenly felt sick at the thought of Finlay comparing her body, and her ways of loving him, with Rose. Oh God, what if he was *unsatisfied* with Ava now that he had shopped around?

'Face it, Ava, if you want Finlay back, you have to *show* him, not tell him. I think you're going to need to rethink your taking it slowly strategy.'

Chapter 34

'What's going on?' Ava asked as Robert opened the door to let her in. 'I had a text from Hazel saying the christening is off. Is Evie not well?'

'No, Evie's fine, sleeping in the nursery at the minute. It's yer woman up there,' he said in exasperation, as he indicated to the bedroom above. 'You better go and have a word with her, see if you can talk some sense into her.'

Ava climbed the staircase and knocked on Hazel's bedroom door. 'Hazel, it's only me, Ava. Can I come in?'

'No, leave me alone.'

'What's going on? You have Evie's christening to get ready for. The guests will be making their way to the church, and we have all that food prepared down in the kitchen.' Ava gently opened the door and peeped in. The curtains were drawn, but she could see Hazel lying in bed, sobbing softly.

Ava ventured in and sat tentatively on the edge of the bed. 'Hazel come on tell me what's wrong?'

'It's nothing to do with Evie,' she wailed.

'What on earth is all this carry on over?' asked Ava.

Hazel sat up, her hair partially twisted around big rollers, the rest of it lying lank and wet around her shoulders. She blew her nose loudly into a tissue. 'I was at the hairdresser's, getting myself ready for Evie's big day. The hairdresser was this new girl, Nicole was her name. Full of chat she was. She asked me if I had a big night out planned, and I says to her, "No, I'm getting ready for a christening." "Whose christening?" she asks and I say, all pleased with myself, my daughter's.' To which, Hazel gulped back a big chest-heaving sob. 'She said, "Oh lovely. Did she have a boy or a girl?"'

Hazel wailed. 'I got up off the chair, with my hair half done, and walked right out. I was scundered. My face tripping me as I walked up the road, with my hair like something the cat dragged through a hedge backwards. The looks I got, I can tell ye, but there was no way I was sitting in that chair to be insulted and expected to pay for the privilege. She thought I was a granny!'

'Oh, sweetheart. She was some stupid wee girl, who didn't have a clue. She couldn't have looked at you right. It's obvious to anyone you don't look like a granny.' Ava wrapped her arms around Hazel. 'Now come on pull yourself together.'

'But what if this is the beginning of it? What if every time I'm in the park with her or standing at the school gates someone thinks I'm her granny. I can't bear it,' she said resuming her noisy sobbing, stopping for a second to blow her nose loudly.

'Oh, come on now, Hazel, wise up. No one looking straight at you would think you're Evie's granny. You look fabulous… Maybe not at the minute, you'd scare the bejaysus out of anyone with the state of you now,' she said trying to make her smile, 'but normally, when you're all done up, and you have your swishy clothes on and your expensive make-up, you look better than anyone I know.'

'Really?' Hazel asked in a small voice, as if desperate to be told she was fit to be presented to the world without being thought of as an old hag.

'Yes, really. Now get out of that bed and wash your face. I'll phone Niamh to come over and finish your hair and she can do your make-up and you'll look fabulous. Then we will get Evie ready in that gorgeous silk christening gown you bought in Dublin and we will have a lovely day.'

Hazel nodded, still sniffing and feeling sorry for herself. 'Thanks, Ava, you're a good friend and I'm glad I asked you to be Evie's godmother. But promise not to tell a soul. It wouldn't do to have them all sniggering about me.'

'Sure, my lips are sealed.'

'And Ava?'

'Yes, Hazel?'

'Robert told me about you and our Ben. I really wouldn't have minded too much about you going out with Ben. You'd have been better than that Mickey any day.'

'He told then?' Ava asked, her face suddenly flushing bright red.

'Oh yes, sure, that big fool of mine couldn't keep a secret from me if his life depended on it.'

Hazel reached over and gave Ava a hug before saying, 'Come on, let's get this show on the road, girl.'

Joseph: *Hey, why no chat lately?*

Ava: *Sorry, just busy. Maggie hasn't been good and I'm trying to do some work to the house. Can't wait for you to see it. Any sign of you taking a holiday and coming home for a while?*

Joseph: *Not likely. There's always some major project on the go and the Americans don't give much holiday leave. You know you can come here any time.*

Ava: *I know. One day. I promise.*

Joseph: *So, what else has been happening?*

Ava: *I'm a godmother now. Hazel asked me to stand for Evie. She's gorgeous.*

Joseph: *Yeah saw the pics on Fake Bake. You looked lovely.*

Ava: *Aww shucks. Thought I'd better make an effort since we were going to the church and all. What time is it there?*

Joseph: *3am.*

Ava: *Why are you not sleeping?*

Joseph: *I don't know. Thinking about you.*

Ava: *Jaysus, that'll give you nightmares.*

Joseph: *So I've discovered.*

Ava: *Go to sleep. I'm away to see Maggie. I'll text you soon. Night night.*

Joseph: *Night, Squid.*

Chapter 35

Ava couldn't imagine Hazel or Niamh putting up with the hardships of living with no central heating and a half-finished kitchen. The bathrooms were in a state and the furnishings were still... well, *unfurnished*. But Ava loved it.

Every morning she woke to the sound of birds twittering away in her garden. She loved opening her back door and stepping out to drink her first cup of coffee of the day, feeling the tender kiss of the early morning air on her face. It didn't matter that the garden was still an overgrown mess, it was her mess and she adored it. The strong scent of the lavender border, almost but not quite overpowering, the more delicate trailing roses competing with the headier earthy smell of moss, all caressed Ava making her feel at ease.

Mount Pleasant Square was beginning to feel like home. When Maggie had moved into the Sisters of Mercy care home, Ava had feared that she would never truly feel at peace again. Seeing her gran's steady decline was heart breaking, but least now there was some sort of shared responsibility with Scarlett.

There was a contentment in Maggie that Ava had never seen before. She wasn't sure if it was borne out of Scarlett's return, or if it was Maggie's awareness that Ava was more settled and happy within herself.

Watching Scarlett and Maggie reacquaint themselves was like seeing two wild bears circle each other, neither wanting to upset the other, in spite of the unspoken accusations hanging around them. Ava accepted that Scarlett would never have the kind of relationship she had experienced with Maggie, and she was sad about that. Somethings could never be fixed, but there was hope. She thought of the Japanese art of kintsugi, whereby broken ceramics were restored, giving them a new lease of life by pouring molten gold or silver into the cracks to hold the pieces together. The broken object becomes a thing of renewed beauty. Maybe Maggie and Scarlett could fashion a new relationship.

The same went for Ava and Finlay. Just because their past relationship had broken didn't mean it was unfixable. Ava was convinced that the break had helped her realise what she wanted out of life. While he was not back on the scene, she felt that it was only a matter of time. She just had to convince him that she was worth having back. That she finally knew her own mind, and that this time, she meant business. She could imagine Maggie admonishing her and saying, 'Sometimes you have to lose something to know it's worth.' She had learnt her lesson. Finlay was everything she needed.

Ava went back to soaking down the wallpaper of the master bedroom walls with a big wet yellow sponge. She was scraping it in preparation for the decorator's arrival the following day and Niamh was supposed to be helping but had claimed to have a sore shoulder resulting from carrying her make-up kit on set the day before.

'I can tell you if you have missed a bit, it is easier to see from over here,' Niamh said from her comfy position tucked into the deep window seat with a pillow behind her back.

'Oh thanks, you're ever so helpful... not,' replied Ava.

'A bit higher and I think that strip will come off in one,' said Niamh indicating to the corner of the yellowing paper which was already peeling away from the wall all on its own. Ava tugged the paper and it came away in one satisfying pull. She didn't mind doing this type of work, especially not when she could see it all coming together at last.

The kitchen was almost finished, the sleek white-coloured units with a granite work surface, replacing the mustard-coloured Formica ones, and stainless-steel appliances finishing it off to create a modern work area. The main living room had been gutted out, the old grey and brown marble fireplace, removed and actually sold for two hundred quid to a salvage yard, had been replaced by a wood burning stove. The old brass light fittings which had hung down looking precarious from a corroding thick chain had been taken out and the wooden floor sanded down, which made the room feel brighter and bigger.

The house was definitely taking shape, and Ava was loving every minute of its transformation. So what if she had sunk every penny she had ever saved into it, and was making mortgage payments that were keeping her awake at night worrying over interest rates, and that she couldn't afford to furnish most of the rooms?

Ninety-seven Mount Pleasant Square was returning her love twofold. She felt energised, excited and happy just being in the house, experiencing its awakening.

'So, what's been happening with you? I haven't seen you for weeks,' said Ava wiping the water-drenched sponge over the wall with firm strokes to soak through the layers of wallpaper.

'Oh, not much, still trying to get my head round losing my dad. I expect that's one that I'll never get used to.'

'Give it time. It's not something you're going to get over, but hopefully you'll be able to remember the good times you had with him,' Ava said.

Niamh nodded. 'I'm back out there trying to distract myself with love.'

'Who is it this time?'

'Colm came back, declaring his marriage was over in all but name, wanting to pick up where he had left off.'

'Please tell me you didn't buy it.' Ava turned with the sodden sponge dripping from her hand.

'No, I did not. I gave him his marching orders. Told him to go back to his family and start behaving like an adult instead of a teenager. Since my dad died, I've sort of felt like I have to behave myself. He could be watching me after all. I just don't want to let myself down and do anything he wouldn't be proud of. So, I was a good girl and told the gorgeous Colm to be on his way.'

'Good for you.'

'And then, the very next day, I started work on the new film being shot down in the Titanic Quarter and discovered I'm working with the loveliest man ever.'

Ava turned to see that Niamh was sparkling; she was all aglow.

'Name and marital status?' asked Ava, indulging her friend's crush.

'He's called Lorcan and he's completely single. I checked up on him before allowing myself to approach him. He's the art director on the set, so he was standing around nearly as much as me between takes. Ava, you have to meet him. He's so funny and smart and interesting. He's worked all over the world, and guess where he's based…'

'Where?' asked Ava, happy to humour her.

'He has a tiny cottage nestled in the Mournes. Isn't that just so quaint? His parents live in Castlewellan so he bought this little old falling down cottage as somewhere to stay when he isn't working.'

'I take it you managed to secure a date with him?' Ava plunged the sponge into the bucket of warm soapy water to attack the next wall.

'No, not yet but I'm working on it. We're back on set tomorrow so I shall be my most entertaining. He seems a bit shy, really, so I don't want to go full on in case I scare him away. Ava this hasn't happened to me in such a long time.'

'Oh please. What hasn't? You're always falling for the latest fella you meet.'

'No, I mean *really* falling for him and for once he isn't someone else's guy.'

'What's he look like then?'

'Curly, dark hair which sort of tumbles about in loose spirals — very Byron. He has the darkest chocolate brown eyes I've ever seen and is at least six feet two and very broad. Oh, he's such a honey, trouble is most of the girls on set think so too.'

'Just be yourself and I'm sure he'll find it hard to resist you. What did Cal make of him?'

'Oh, he didn't see what the rest of us were twittering on about. Said he looked a bit up himself.'

'I'm just glad you had enough sense to send Colm on his way. You really are selling yourself short when you get involved with married men. Apart from the rights and wrongs of it all, you inevitably end up hurt. It's a game no one wins.'

'I know, I know. I've made a few mistakes, but honestly, I feel so different about everything to do with men now. I don't know why I let myself get involved with the wrong ones so often, but unless I know without a doubt that someone is unattached, then I'm not even going to get into a conversation with them. Suppose I'm growing up.'

''Bout time,' said Ava reaching to scrape away a corner piece which was resisting her tugging. 'You were beginning to act like the oldest teenager in town.'

'Oh, thanks. Glad to know you think so highly of me. Still, I know I've messed around for too long. It's time to stop selling myself short and if Lorcan isn't the right one then I will just have to wait it out until he turns up,' Niamh said readjusting the cushion behind her head.

'Listen to you, sounding all sure of yourself. Wait till you're blootered some night and find yourself sitting on the lap of some handsome banker with a wedding band and two kids.'

'No honestly, I can't live with all that drama any more. I want my dad to know that I'm making good choices, and I think he'd like Lorcan, which is more than I can say for most of the other men I've ever been involved with.'

'Good for you. I hope the poor fella knows what he's getting into with you.'

'Oh, don't fret. He'll have no complaints if I get to have my wicked way with him.' She settled back into the cosy nest she had created for herself on the window seat. 'I'm going to take a wee snooze for half an hour. Wake me up when you're done.'

Chapter 36

The scent of autumn leaves, burning in a bonfire, hung in the air, reminding Ava that time was rushing on. She worried that every visit to see Maggie could be her last. It was hard to see Maggie decline, she was sleeping more and eating less. Her periods of lucid chat were becoming less frequent, but yet, there was still a sense of serenity and peacefulness around her, which Ava took comfort from.

Ava smiled to herself as she watched Scarlett and Quinn, the gardener at the Sisters of Mercy care home, chat away. They were relaxed and clearly enjoying each other's company, looking like they had known each other for years.

Quinn was laughing at Scarlett, his face completely altered from the surly, serious expression he normally wore. Ava noticed he had grown a beard which suited him. Scott, his equally quiet and surly fifteen-year-old son, was lifting huge armfuls of cut grass and carrying it to a pile at the bottom of the garden to the bonfire.

Ava looked over to Maggie. Her soft white curls were tidy and orderly and her skin, though lined by time, still glowed. Scarlett's version of Maggie as a tyrant — who had tried hard to crush her talent, had resented her freedom and belittled her achievements — didn't add up for Ava. None of it rang true, but still Ava hadn't wanted to openly call her mother a liar. If that was her take on growing up in Moonstone Street then she could hardly deny Scarlett her version of the truth.

Ava liked to think of herself as being the fortunate one. Maggie's love and attention had never wavered, nor waned. She had cared for Ava with the dedication of the best of mothers and for this, Ava would be eternally grateful. When Scarlett had mocked Ava for her devotion to Maggie and had sniped about needing to loosen the apron strings before they hung her, she had bristled, but bit her tongue and decided that they needed more time to understand each other. She didn't want to judge Scarlett too harshly and was quietly desperate for Scarlett to like and accept her.

Ava's reverie was broken by humming drifting in through the window. It was a familiar tune, but Ava couldn't have named it.

Later, on the way home, Ava thought of the song and asked Scarlett had she been humming one of her own songs while in the garden.

'Oh, I do it without even knowing I'm doing it, sometimes. Yes, it's "Black Bird Fly Away"' Then she sang a couple of lines:

Black bird, fly through my dreams,
Lift me from the ether and take me to new lands.
Let me feel your wings spread beneath me
As I soar high and higher.

Ava was spellbound, Scarlett's voice had an eerie, mystical quality which was hypnotising. For the first time, she had a sense of what Scarlett's talent must have been like and glimpsed the effect she must have had over her audience.

The past few weeks had been fraught with emotion, both mother and daughter desperate to build some sort of meaningful relationship out of their bond. But it wasn't easy. Ava found herself making excuses for Scarlett's selfish ways, her constant need to be talking about the wonderful life she had in America, her elaborate stories of her days playing in the band, and the friends she had left behind in LA. Sometimes Ava just wanted to say, get over yourself, either be here with me and Maggie, or pack up your hippy shit and head on back to LA if it is so bloody wonderful. But of course, she didn't dare say anything for fear of losing her again. Ava was willing to put up with all her faults to just have some sort of relationship with her.

Chapter 37

'Hello, Mom. How are you doing?' asked Scarlett, her American accent sounding out of place in the convent home.

Ava kissed Maggie on the forehead and straightened up her pillow. The last few weeks had been hard. Maggie appeared to have given up the will to live. She was eating little and seemed to be in a world of her own more and more. Ava queried whether she should be moved to a hospital, but the GP, Doctor Napier had said she was better off where she was being cared for by the calm and even-tempered nuns and attendants. A bustling hospital ward would disorientate her further, and there was no guarantee she wouldn't pick up one of the more-serious bugs.

Sister Lucy had promised to ring Ava, day or night, if there was any change. She lived with her mobile phone attached to her at all times, just in case.

Scarlett sat on the edge of the bed looking restless already. She seemed to have no sense of staying still and just being. It was another fault which irritated Ava. It was as if Scarlett was always looking for something better to do.

'Do you want to take a walk up to the communal kitchen and make a cup of tea?' asked Ava, willing Scarlett to give her some time alone with Maggie. Since Scarlett had come home, Ava had felt off key with her relationship with Maggie. At times, Ava felt Scarlett displaced her, that Ava was no longer Maggie's number one priority. Ridiculous she knew, considering poor Maggie was lying in a bed unable to look after either of them or make a hint of suggestion as to which was her preferred child. The truth was, meeting Scarlett had only served to make Ava feel more like

Maggie's child than ever before. She shared more of Maggie's stoic personality than that of Scarlett's fiery restlessness.

Scarlett's sense of entitlement also agitated her; it was as if she expected people to greet her like the prodigal daughter, welcoming her back with open arms despite her having been away for years without any contact. Even Sister Lucy had rejoiced to see mother and daughter reunited, as if to say Maggie could die in peace at last. But Ava wasn't ready to let Maggie go, and almost saw Scarlett's presence as pushing her on.

Still, Ava knew she was perhaps being a bit harsh. Scarlett was trying hard to forge some sort of relationship with her. The trouble was that neither of them had much in common. Even the things they shared, like growing up in Moonstone Street were divisive. While Ava had nothing but warm, happy memories of a childhood suffused in love, Scarlett saw Moonstone Street as a claustrophobic brick box which she had longed to escape along with the iron grip of her parents.

Ava also assumed that Scarlett considered her life to be parochial, verging on plain boring. While Scarlett had spent her twenties travelling all over America in a custom-built tour bus packed with her four band members and a succession of cute, muscled roadies, Ava was busy working in Blooming Dales while trying to keep Moonstone Street ticking over, overseeing the building work on number ninety-seven looking after Maggie.

Scarlett stood up and stretched elaborately as if she had been sitting still for hours. 'Yes, I'll go fetch a cup of coffee. How about you, Ava, would you like one?'

'No thanks, I'm fine,' replied Ava, a touch tetchy.

Scarlett flounced off, oblivious to Ava's irritation.

'Gran, how are you today?' Ava asked.

Maggie didn't flicker. She lay as still as a log felled in a forest.

'Must be nice for you to know Scarlett's around again. Still, she can be a tad wearing. Sometimes I think I will scream if she doesn't stop humming her bloody songs, expecting us all to listen and applaud. Yes, I know you'd probably tell me to stop moaning and be more grateful that she has come back, but the truth is I think I liked the idea of her better than the reality.' Ava giggled as she realised how true that was.

'Don't preach, Gran. I know that I should be nice to her and I am, I just need to offload a little in case I snap, and under duress say something about her hair, her clothes, or her phoney American accent.'

Ava could have sworn she saw a flicker of amusement pass over Maggie's immobile face. Just a twitch, but she looked like Ava's predicament was humouring her. *God, I'm imagining things now*, thought Ava.

'Move over, Gran, I think you need to let me in beside you.' Ava joked. She used to love sleeping next to Maggie, though it only happened rarely when she was sick or on Christmas Eve.

'God, I feel so guilty,' said Scarlett later, as they made their way home.

Ava nodded in agreement. 'I know, every time I leave her there I feel like I should run back and kidnap her. It doesn't seem right to walk away and leave her just lying there.'

'No, not about Mom, about *you*. I feel so bad that I've left you to do all *this*,' she said, waving her hands expressively as if to take in the entirety of the Sisters of Mercy care home and Ava's life.

'What?' asked Ava looking at her, trying to fathom what she was on about.

'You shouldn't have had to look after my mom. You should have been living your life, not caring for an elderly relative.'

'I don't think of Gran as just an elderly relative. I want to care for her. She isn't a burden to be escaped from you know.' Ava was bristling with indignation.

'Didn't you long to escape? To live a different life from this? You shouldn't be shackled to an old woman at your age.'

There it was again that: that implication that life here wasn't good enough. Ava was sick of it. Sick of Scarlett comparing Belfast to LA, sick of her insinuating that her life was so much more fulfilled than Ava's could ever be. Who was Scarlett to swan into their lives and make judgements like that?

'God, you are so full of yourself. Have you ever considered anyone else or has it always been about your needs, your desires?' Ava could feel the heat rising up her neck to her face. She was flushed crimson, her anger manifest. It wasn't like Ava to cause a scene or even voice an opinion strongly. She firmly believed in live and let live and didn't seek to force her views on anyone else. But this time, Ava was pushed to the limit.

Scarlett turned and looked directly at Ava. 'Reel it back, babe. I'm only thinking of you. There's more to life than visiting a retirement home every night and working in a florist's shop. Didn't you have dreams? Ambitions?'

'Some of us are just happy to be. There doesn't have to be another life waiting out there. Why can't you see I'm not like you and everything you hated about Maggie you may as well hate about me, because I have more in common with her than I will ever have with you.' Ava stopped. She was breathless, spent. Why was she bothering? Scarlett wouldn't understand the bond she had with Maggie. There was no point in trying to explain her life to her.

They drove on in silence. The sharp, cold air around them a reminder of the sea of pain between them.

Chapter 38

'You're right, of course,' said Scarlett that night, 'It does look like I've lived my life to please myself, and to an extent that's true.' They were sitting in the living room with the television on low even though neither of them had any interest in the latest search-for-a-star competition.

'It doesn't matter to me. What's happened has happened. We all make choices, some good some bad. It's not for me to judge you. For what it's worth, I wouldn't have changed my life for anything,' Ava replied, glad to have a chance to clear the air.

They had been avoiding this conversation for weeks.

'Yeah, I can see that. Maggie probably did a better job than I ever could have.'

Scarlett paused for a second as if to consider what she said next.

Ava waited not wanting to pander to her need for reassurance. She didn't deserve to have her scant conscience considered.

'Things were different then. Living during the Troubles was like having a life suspended. There was fear in everything we did, yet we didn't know it. It wasn't until I had moved to England that I realised what we had put up with. The constant incendiary atmosphere, knowing at any time there could be a bomb or a shooting. Your granddad worked for the Water Board and being one of the very few Catholics made him a target. I used to worry myself sick that something would happen to him. Then as I hit my teenage years it was easier to pull away from him and resent his choices rather than worry for him. I used to want to shake him and say why do you put up with it? He would be tormented by the other Protestant workers, had to watch them get better jobs, bigger pay packets and there was nothing he could do about it. Speak up and you risked getting a bullet. But I was too young and naive to accept that fate, which he so stoically resigned himself to.

'For me, the choice was simple, I had to get out. I couldn't bare the constant burr of the helicopters overhead, watching everyone, looking for trouble. It felt like they wished it upon us. The British soldiers in the streets, squatting down with their guns aimed at you as you walked by, the RUC Land Rovers patrolling the streets, the searches every time you walked into a shop in town. It was a different way of living than now. I felt strangled by it and needed to escape. Except, I found that everywhere has its restrictions. They often just come in different guises.'

Ava let her talk. Listening to Scarlett's version of how her life had been — it was like reading the other side of Maggie's letter. Neither mother nor daughter understood or appreciated each other, and Ava was the conduit between them, reading between the lines.

Ava still found it hard to believe that after all this time Scarlett was here with her. She cast a glance at her, drinking in her profile. She was still an attractive woman. Her skin was the colour of Bailey's Irish cream, smooth and creamy. Her nose, different from Ava's own, was short and turned upwards making her look slightly mischievous and impish. Her hair was shoulder length and the colour of truffles, with a kinky, curly texture which never seemed to stay the same two days in a row, and her mouth was full and sensuous.

It was strange to feel such an intense bond with a virtual stranger. Just because she knew they were biologically connected, that she was born of this woman, she had felt an instant kinship. Ava tried to imagine if she could have picked her out of a crowd, but the truth was she probably couldn't have. Nevertheless, knowing that she was her mother was enough to melt any reserves clean away. In all honesty, she had to admit that she wanted to form a relationship with her and so she tried as best she could to accommodate her at every turn.

When Scarlett looked for forgiveness, Ava gave it unconditionally. She told her she could understand her predicament, the call of her music career and the shackles of caring for a newborn baby were not compatible. Ava had made it easy for Scarlett to fit right on into her life. But really, when she lay alone in bed at night, she quaked with disappointment and anger. How could she have walked out on her so completely? Letters, gifts and visits she could count on one hand up until she turned seven were not the stuff of good parenting by any stretch of the imagination.

'So, I was really meant to be called Ruby?' Ava asked later that night as they shared a glass of wine and ate some spicy chicken with rice and a green salad that Scarlett had prepared earlier that day.

Scarlett smiled as she set her wine glass down on the table. 'Yep, actually to begin with I wanted to call you Ruby Tuesday, since you were born on a Tuesday and then when I got to know you a little better I discovered you were such a solemn little being, all serious and worried looking that I though Ruby Blue would suit you. But knowing I would have to show my face back home eventually and have the show down with my mother and father, I opted for Ruby Ava with Ava being my grandmother's name.'

Ava laughed. God, to think she could have been Ruby Blue, what a moniker.

'It's strange that since you have come back and I've learnt so much about you and in turn myself, I sort of feel more like Ruby than Ava.'

'Go with it. Embrace who you are and who you want to be.'

Ava laughed. 'You're starting to sound all Oprah again. Remember you are in Belfast now, not California,' she chided.

Ava knew that at times Scarlett could scarcely believe that she was home. 'I just mean that we don't have to stay in the same role all our lives. Change can come along or we can instigate it ourselves. Don't limit yourself.'

Ava helped herself to more chicken. 'You know, maybe I do need to be more open to possibilities.'

'I'd say that would be a perfect toast.' Scarlett raised her glass. 'To possibilities.'

'To possibilities,' Ava echoed, smiling at her mother thinking of the chance she was ready to take to get Finlay back.

Chapter 39

Ava was woken by Lulu pawing at her arm and meowing. The cat wanted to be let out, to explore the gardens. Fragments of dreams drifted through Ava's mind as she pulled back the duvet. She had been dreaming of Joseph and Finlay. They had been competing to win her a giant squid stuffed toy at a fairground. Each jostling the other out of the way to throw wooden hoops around rotating skittles. The cat had woken her before she had discovered the winner.

Ava walked down the stairs, the cat at her heels, thinking about Finn. She was prepared to put the work into their relationship. Now that she had nearly won him back, things would have to be different. She wouldn't take him for granted. She let Lulu out and filled the kettle, before popping some bread into the toaster. Breakfast in the garden would be lovely, she decided. But first she texted Finlay to remind him to meet her at one o'clock at French Village on Botanic Avenue. After lunch and she would bring him back to Mount Pleasant Square, to show him around, and then hopefully they would pick up where they'd left off.

Just then her phone pinged. She glanced down expecting it to be Finn's reply and saw it was Joseph.

Hey, Ava. Fed up with you refusing to fly out to me. I've booked a ticket. Coming home. I miss you. I miss your voice, your stupid jokes and even the way you cheat at Scrabble. For the record, millimeum is not a word.

Will see you soon. Joseph. X

She read the text again, and in that instant, something jolted within her. A knowing, so deep and powerful, that it frightened her. Joseph. Her friend, her constant in life, when all else seemed to be in disarray. She had scarcely allowed herself to ever think of him as anything other than her friend, but she knew she thought of him often, if not every single day. There were weeks when they texted constantly, then times when it wasn't so frequent. But that contact, that need to hear from him, was always there. She thought back over their last messages to each other. It was there, like a whisper or a promise unspoken, but actual and real. A suggestion of something else.

The previous year had seen her change and grow. Maggie's decline, the inheritance, meeting Scarlett – it had all changed something inside Ava. Her relationship with Ben had awakened a longing she hadn't known before. But as fun as it was, she knew Ben wasn't right. Then Finn, and the thought of him with Rose, was enough to convince her that she wanted him back. She thought of all her messages to Joseph; the jokes that only they shared, the shorthand way they could read each other's mood though thousands of miles apart. How he had been supportive of her need to care for Maggie, how he understood their bond, how he had witnessed their closeness over the years. In all the time she had known him, he had never made a move on her, but then she had been with Finlay.

Now she was single, and Joseph was coming home.

Ava stood with the phone still in her hand and replied.

Mount Pleasant Square is almost habitable. Your room awaits. x

THE END

Acknowledgments

This book is dedicated to all the wonderful women in my life: my mum Jeannie, my grannies Kitty and Violet, my aunt Marilyn, my sisters Lyndsey and Kim, my cousin Jennifer, sisters-in-law Patricia, Janeen, Anne and Anita, and my daughters Kate and Sarah.

Thanks also goes to my friends: Deborah, Zoe, Tracey, Joanne, Andrea, Joan, Katie, Roma, Janette, and Donna, and all the wonderful writer friends who have supported me along the way, especially Women Aloud NI and Kelly Creighton.

Thanks also to writers Claire Allan and Fionnuala Cassidy for the encouragement and support. You girls are stars! I am grateful to the wonderful Pat Hamilton and Neil Ranasinghe for picking up typos.

Special praise to the amazing Bombshell team: Betsy, Fred, Alexina, Sumaria, Sarah and Morgen and the network of fantastic bloggers and reviewers.

Thanks to Liam and never forgetting Owen.

Lightning Source UK Ltd.
Milton Keynes UK
UKHW01f0800270718
326385UK00001B/125/P